"I Don't Know What To Do With You," Drew Muttered.

She rested her forehead on his collarbone. "I have a few ideas."

Her droll humor startled a laugh from him. "I hope we're on the same page."

Her answer was to kiss him sweetly. Breathing heavily, he stepped away, trying to elude temptation. "I think one of us is supposed to say this is going too fast."

She shrugged, leaning back on her hands. "I've had a terrible crush on you for over a year, even when you were being an obnoxious, overbearing plutocrat."

"Ouch." His wince was not feigned. Hearing her description of his less-than-stellar qualities made him squirm. "I thought we called a truce."

"Under duress and the threat of apocalypse."

"Then I'll say it again," he muttered quietly. "For the moment, I'm not going to fight with you or try to make you see reason."

She crooked a finger. He went to her like a kite on a string, hoping she didn't recognize the hold she had on him.

* * *

Stranded with the Rancher is a Texas Cattleman's Club: After the Storm novel—As a Texas town rebuilds, love heals all wounds...

* * *

If you're on Twitter,
tell us what you think of Harlequin Desire!
#harlequindesire

Dear Reader,

In April of 2009, my husband and I traveled to Murfreesboro, Tennessee, to visit family for Easter weekend. Saturday, a hot and muggy day, we went out for lunch. The steakhouse we chose had a bank of televisions over the bar area.

As we ate our meal, we glanced again and again at the weather maps covered with yellow, orange and—most sinister of all—red areas. Storms were popping up all over the South.

At the time, however, nothing was happening exactly where we were...not even rain. After lunch, we planned to hit the grocery store to stock up on food for the next day's lunch. The women said we should go home. The men said we had time to do our errand first.

We piled into the car, turned left out of the parking lot, and immediately saw something pretty darned terrifying. A funnel cloud dropped out of the sky.

Imagine a lot of yelling and throwing the car into Reverse. We, along with a crowd of other people, ran back into the restaurant and huddled in the restrooms. We stayed there a very long time, not really knowing when it was safe to head back outside.

Later, we saw the damage. An F4 tornado, half a mile wide, had stayed on the ground for twenty-two miles. Miraculously, there were fewer than five fatalities.

That memory was very much in my mind as I wrote *Stranded with the Rancher.* In the future, though, I'd rather not do my research quite so thoroughly!

Have fun with this first installment of Texas Cattleman's Club: After the Storm. Thanks for reading. ☺

Janice Maynard

STRANDED WITH THE RANCHER

JANICE MAYNARD

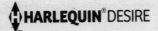
HARLEQUIN® DESIRE

Special thanks and acknowledgment are given to Janice Maynard for her contribution to the Texas Cattleman's Club: After the Storm miniseries.

Recycling programs
for this product may
not exist in your area.

ISBN-13: 978-0-373-73342-2

Stranded with the Rancher

Copyright © 2014 by Harlequin Books S.A.

Printed in U.S.A.

HARLEQUIN®
www.Harlequin.com

Books by Janice Maynard

Harlequin Desire

The Billionaire's Borrowed Baby #2109
*Into His Private Domain #2135
*A Touch of Persuasion #2146
*Impossible to Resist #2164
*The Maid's Daughter #2182
*All Grown Up #2206
*Taming the Lone Wolff #2236
*A Wolff at Heart #2260
A Billionaire for Christmas #2271
Beneath the Stetson #2276
§A Not-So-Innocent Seduction #2296
Baby for Keeps #2307
Stranded with the Rancher #2329

Silhouette Desire

The Secret Child & the Cowboy CEO #2040

*The Men of Wolff Mountain
§The Kavanaghs of Silver Glen

Other titles by this author available in ebook format.

JANICE MAYNARD

is a *USA TODAY* bestselling author who lives in beautiful east Tennessee with her husband. She holds a B.A. from Emory and Henry College and an M.A. from East Tennessee State University. In 2002 Janice left a fifteen-year career as an elementary school teacher to pursue writing full-time. Now her first love is creating sexy, character-driven, contemporary romance stories.

Janice loves to travel and enjoys using those experiences as settings for books. Hearing from readers is one of the best perks of the job! Visit her website, www.janicemaynard.com, and follow her on Facebook and Twitter.

To police, fire and rescue personnel who rush in during times of chaos to keep us all safe...thank you for what you do....

One

Drew Farrell glanced at the sky. Storm clouds roiled and twisted, setting his mood on edge. He shoved the truck's gearshift into park, jammed his Stetson on his head and strode across the road. Dust billowed with each angry step, coating his hand-tooled cowboy boots.

Deliberately, he crossed the line that separated his property from his neighbor's. Beth Andrews. His beautiful, long-legged, sexy-as-hell neighbor. After two years of butting heads with her at regular intervals, you'd think he would be immune to her considerable physical appeal.

But no. Her naturally curly blond hair and green eyes hit his libido at a weak spot. Sadly, there was no twelve-step program for men wanting women who drove them nuts.

He approached Beth's organic produce stand and ground his teeth when he saw she had multiple customers waiting. Cooling his heels, jaw clenched, he courted patience. But he wanted to lambast her with righteous indignation while his temper was hot.

Like every day recently, at least a dozen cars had parked haphazardly up and down the private lane, causing congestion and spooking Drew's prize-winning thoroughbreds in the adjoining pasture. This morning, his men had been forced to move seven horses to a grassy field on the opposite side of his property, for no other reason than because Beth had started selling pumpkins.

Pumpkins, for God's sake. The traffic she had created during the summer—selling squash and tomatoes and a dozen other vegetables—had increased tenfold since she'd put up signs all over Royal advertising fall harvest decorations. At least during the summer months the crowd was spread out. But come October first, it was as if everyone within a fifty-mile radius of Drew's ranch had decided they *had* to buy one of Beth's fat, healthy pumpkins for their porches.

As Drew waited impatiently, several of the patrons loaded up their purchases and drove away. Finally, only one woman remained—a young blonde. Very pregnant. From what Drew could tell, she had picked out the largest pumpkin she could find. Beth and the customer squatted to lift the pumpkin from its perch on a bale of hay. The big, orange orb slipped out of their hands, nearly rolling onto their feet.

Oh, good grief. Snapping out of his funk, Drew strode forward, determined to stop them before somebody got hurt. The thing must weigh forty pounds.

"Let me do that," he said, elbowing them out of the way. "One of you has a baby to consider and you, Ms. Andrews, ought to know better." The spark of surprise and irritation in Beth's eyes made him want to grin despite his surly mood. The pregnant woman's car sat only a few feet away in the handicapped parking spot. For Halloween, Beth had designated the space beside the shed with a sign and a skeleton holding a crutch. She was creative—he'd give her that.

Hefting the pumpkin with ease, he set it gently in the trunk. Fortunately, the base of the thing was pretty flat.

Given its weight, there was little chance it would roll over unless the driver made a reckless turn.

The customer smiled at him. "Thanks for your help." Unlike Beth's sunshiny curls, this woman's straight blond hair was so fair it was almost white. Her skin was pale as well. Despite her advanced pregnancy, she was thin, almost frail.

He dusted his hands on his pants. "No problem. Get someone to help you lift that thing when you get home."

"I will." She paused, one handing resting protectively on her rounded abdomen. "I always loved Halloween as a kid. I thought it would be fun this year to carve a jack-o'-lantern for my daughter and put pictures of it in her baby book."

Beth glanced at the woman's belly. "Are you due that soon?"

"No. I have another eight or nine weeks to go. But she's already a person to me. I talk to her all the time. I guess that sounds crazy."

"Not at all."

Beth's smile struck Drew as wistful. Maybe if her biological clock ticked loud enough, she'd meet some guy and move away. Then Drew could buy the land she had stolen from him. Oddly, that notion was not as appealing as it should have been.

Beth spoke up again. "Who's your master carver? The baby's dad?"

A flash of anguish darkened the woman's eyes, but it was gone so quickly Drew thought he might have imagined it. "*I'm* going to do it. I'm trained in graphic design, so this is right up my alley. I should go," she said, as if suddenly realizing that the weather was going downhill fast. "Don't want to get caught in the rain."

Drew stood shoulder to shoulder with Beth as they

watched the car disappear into the distance. "Did she look familiar to you?" he asked, frowning.

"Maybe. Why?"

"I don't know. Just an odd feeling that I might have seen her before."

At that moment, a strong gust of wind snatched the plastic banner and ripped it off the top of Beth's produce stand. The bright green lettering spelled out GREEN ACRES. Drew seldom had time to watch TV, but even *he* got the reference to the old sitcom where the wealthy Manhattan couple moved to the country and bought a farm. It was easy to imagine Beth wearing an evening gown and heels. She was tall for a woman, at least five seven. But Drew had half a dozen inches or more on her.

He helped her capture the surprisingly heavy sign and roll it up. "You might as well put it away for now," he said. "The wind is not going to die down anytime soon."

When they had stashed the sign beneath a plywood counter, Beth shook her head and stared at him. "I'd be happy to sell you a pumpkin, Drew, but somehow, I don't think that's why you're here."

The derision in her voice made it sound as if he were the most boring guy on the planet. "I decorate the ranch for fall," he said, wincing inwardly when he heard the defensive note in his voice.

"Correction. You have *people* who do that for you. It's not the same thing at all, Drew."

He'd grown accustomed to her barbs. In fact, if he were honest, he occasionally enjoyed their heated spats. Beth gave as good as she got. He liked that in a woman. Now, when he didn't shoot back immediately with a retort, she watched him with a wary gaze, her arms wrapped around her waist in a cautious posture.

The tint of her green eyes was nothing as simple as

grass or emerald. They were an unusual mix of shades, shot through with tinges of amber and gold. The color reminded him of a prize marble he'd had as a kid. He still kept the little ball of glass as a good luck charm in his dresser. Perhaps that was why he had so much trouble getting Beth out of his head. Every day when he reached in the drawer to grab a pair of socks, he saw that beautiful marble.

"Earth to Drew. If you're not buying anything, please leave."

Every time she pursed her lips in that disapproving schoolmarm fashion, he wanted to kiss her. Even when he was mad as hell. Today was no different. But today he was determined to get a few things ironed out.

Glaring at her with his best intimidating frown, he spoke firmly. "You have to relocate your produce stand. The traffic jams spook my horses, block the road and besides...." He pulled up short, about to voice something best left unsaid.

Beth's shoulder-length hair danced in the breeze, the curls swirling and tangling. It gave her a just-out-of-bed look that was not helping him in his determination to be businesslike and resolute.

"Besides what?" she asked sharply. "Spit it out."

He hesitated. But what the hell... He and Beth shared the road. She might as well know where he was coming from. "My clientele is high-end. When they come to Willowbrook Farms to drop several million dollars on a thoroughbred that might have a shot at the Triple Crown, your little set-up here gives the wrong impression. It's like having a lemonade stand on the steps of a major banking institution. Your business is frivolous, mine is not."

Beth absorbed his words with a pang of regret. Virtually everybody in town liked Drew Farrell and thought of him as a decent down-to-earth guy. He was an important member of the Texas Cattleman's Club. Membership in the TCC—an elite enclave where the wealthy ranchers of Royal met to broker deals, kick back, relax and count their millions—was a privilege and a lifelong commitment. Not that Beth really knew what went on behind those hallowed doors, but she could imagine. Which meant that Beth, who saw Drew as arrogant and self-important, was out of step with the rest of the county. For whatever reason, she and Drew were the proverbial oil and water.

But he'd just exposed the root of the matter. His lineage was impeccable. He was blue-blooded old money, while she came from near-poverty, part of a family line that was crooked on its best days.

"If the traffic is such a big deal to you, put a road in somewhere else."

"There *is* nowhere else," he said, his jaw carved in stone. "My plan two years ago was to buy this land we're standing on and put a beautiful white fence along both sides of the road. A Kentucky horse farm look, minus the bluegrass. But you stole it out from under me."

"I didn't steal anything," she said patiently, hiding her glee that for once in her life she had staged a coup. "You lowballed the guy because you thought nobody else wanted it. I merely had the good sense to make a reasonable offer. He accepted. End of story. I might point out that you're trespassing."

The wind had really kicked up now. Even so, the heat was oppressive. The sky changed colors in rapid succession...one moment angry gray, the next a sickly green.

Beth glanced toward Drew's property, feeling her skin tighten with unease. "Have you listened to a weather forecast?" she asked. It wasn't a deliberate attempt to change the subject. She was concerned. Normally, she would keep the shed open until four-thirty at least, but today she wanted to batten down the hatches and be tucked up in her cozy two-bedroom bungalow before the first raindrop fell.

In the time since she purchased the farm, she had updated the inside of the cute little house and made it her own. If Drew had bought the property, he probably would have bulldozed the place. The farmhouse was old, but Beth loved it. Not only was it a wonderful home, it was concrete proof that she had made something of her life.

She had a knack for growing things. The Texas soil was rich and fertile. She wasn't going to let a self-important billionaire push her around. Drew had been born into money, but his horse breeding enterprise had added to the coffers substantially.

Now Drew's gaze scanned the sky as well. "The radio said we have a tornado watch, but I doubt it will be too bad. We're a little bit out of the usual path for storms like that. Haven't had one in years. Even when we do, the ones that do the damage tend to happen in the spring, not the fall. I don't think you have anything to worry about."

"I hope not."

"So back to my original point," he said. "Your little enterprise here is adversely affecting my business. If we can't come to some kind of amicable solution, I'll have to involve the county planning board."

"Are you actually threatening me?" She looked at him askance.

His wording made her heart race. In some perverse way, she got a charge out of their frequent heated arguments. Despite his suborn refusal to acknowledge her right to operate her produce stand as she saw fit, she was secretly attracted to him, much against her better judgment.

Although most days she would be more than happy to wring Drew Farrell's wealthy, entitled neck, she couldn't discount the fact that he was 100 percent grade A prime beef. That probably wasn't a politically correct description, but seriously, the man was incredibly handsome. He wore his dark brown hair a little on the shaggy side. The untamed look suited him, though. And his bright blue eyes had probably been getting females into trouble since he graduated from kindergarten.

She knew he had been engaged once in his mid-twenties. Something happened to break it off, so Drew had been a free agent for the last six or seven years. He was a mover and shaker in Royal, Texas. In short, everything Beth was not.

She didn't have a chip on her shoulder about her upbringing. More like a large splinter, really. But it didn't take a genius to see that she and Drew were not at all suited. Still, it was difficult to ignore his physical appeal.

His eyes narrowed. "It's not a threat, Beth. But I'll do whatever I have to in order to protect my investments. It's worth it to me to restore peace and quiet to this road, to my life for that matter."

"So mature and staid," she mocked.

"I'm only four years older than you," he snapped.

His knowledge surprised her. "Be reasonable, Drew. I have as much right to be here as you do. True, I may be David to your Goliath. But if you remember your Sunday school lessons, that didn't end well for the giant."

"Now who's threatening whom?"

For the first time, a nuance of humor lightened his expression. But it was gone so quickly it was possible she imagined it. He was definitely spoiling for a fight. If it weren't for her splitting headache caused by the change in weather, she would be more inclined to oblige him.

She really did understand his frustration. As a horse breeder, Drew's reputation was world-renowned. He sold beautiful, competitive animals to movie stars, sheikhs, and many other eccentric wealthy patrons. Her modest organic farming operation must drive him berserk.

But why should *she* have to suffer? Her small house and a few acres of land were all she had in the world. She'd worked hard to get them.

"Plant some trees," she said. "Fast-growing ones. You really should quit harassing me. I might have to get a re-straining order or something."

She was kidding, of course. But her humor fell flat. Drew was not amused. "I don't think you understand how serious I am about this. There's a road on the far side of your place. Why can't customers come to the produce stand that way?"

Hands on hips, she glared at him. "It's a cattle path, not a road. It would take thousands of dollars to improve it, and in case you haven't noticed, I'm not the one with the silver spoon in my mouth."

His gaze was stormy. "Why did you want this particu-lar piece of land anyway?"

She shrugged, unable to fully explain the emotions that had overtaken her when she realized she could finally af-ford a place of her own. "It was the right size and the right price. And I fell in love with it."

"You can't run a serious business based on feelings."

"Wanna bet?" His patronizing attitude began to get on her nerves. "Why don't you tell your elite clients that I'm a sharecropper, and you're doing your good deed for the year?"

"That's not funny."

Earlier, she had picked up an inkling of humor from him. Now he looked like he would sooner murder her in her sleep than make a joke.

"I have two whole fields of pumpkins ready to sell,"

she said. "And a third bunch not far behind. I'll make enough money this month to keep my books in the black during the winter. Lucky for you, a horse is still a horse in the middle of January. But my farm will be cold and dead until spring."

"You're fighting a losing battle. In this economy, you can't hope to survive long term. And in the meantime, you're creating enormous problems for me."

Fury tightened her throat. She had struggled her entire life to make something of herself, against pretty long odds. To have Drew dismiss the fruits of her labor with such careless male superiority told her he had no clue who she really was.

"Maybe I'll fail," she said, her tone as dispassionate as she could make it. "And maybe I won't. But I'm like Scarlett O'Hara in *Gone With the Wind*. I read the book when I was thirteen. Even then, I understood what her father told her. Land is what's important. Land is the only thing that lasts."

Drew rubbed his eyes with the heels of his hands, probably to keep from strangling her. "That makes perfect sense," he said quietly, "*if* this had been in your family's possession for generations. But it's *not* Andrews land. And I freely admit that it's *not* Farrell land either. It does, however, adjoin my property, Beth."

"If you were so hell bent on having it, you should have outbid me." They squabbled frequently about her supposed infractions of the "neighbor" code, but this was the first time he'd been so visibly angry. She knew that at the heart of the matter was his desire to buy her out, though he hadn't mentioned it today. The last time he'd tried, she'd accused him of harassment.

"I'm merely asking you to see reason."

His implication that she was *un*reasonable made her

grind her teeth. "I think we'll have to agree to disagree on this one."

"Will you at least consider selling your produce somewhere in town? If you think about it, the central location could increase your customer base and it would keep the traffic off this road."

Darn him, he had a point. But she wasn't willing to cede the field yet. Her involuntary mental pun might have made her laugh if she hadn't been in the midst of a heated argument with her macho, gorgeous neighbor. "Part of the experience of coming to Green Acres is for tourists and locals to *see* the pumpkins in the field. They can take pictures to their heart's content and post them on Facebook. If they want to, they can traipse around the lot and choose their own prize. The ambience would be totally different in town."

Drew knew when to back off strategically. He had given her something to think about. For the moment. But he wasn't going to give up. Horse breeding was a long-term venture. Patience and planning and persistence made the difference. Of course, a little dollop of luck now and then didn't hurt either.

Beth was stubborn and passionate. He could respect that. "I tell you what," he said. "If you think about my suggestion and decide you could sell in bigger quantities in town, my guys will help you get set up, including all the logistics of hauling your stuff. Does that sound fair?" He paused. "You can have as much time as you need to think about it."

She tugged at a strand of hair the wind had whipped into her mouth. He couldn't help noticing her lips. They were pink and perfect. Eminently kissable. He wondered if her lip gloss was flavored. The random thought caught him off guard. He was in the midst of a serious conflict, not an intimate proposition. Though the latter had definite appeal.

Beth stared at him, her expression hard to fathom. "Do you always get what you want?" she asked quietly.

Guilt pinched hard. His life had been golden up until this point. He had a hunch Beth's had not. "It's not a sin to go after what you want," he muttered.

"Exactly," she said. "And that's what I did when I bought my home. You had a chance, but you made a poor business decision. You can't blame me for that."

Drew noticed in some unoccupied corner of his mind that the wind was no longer as wild. The air was thick and moist. Sweat trickled down his back. Beth, however, looked cool and comfortable in a navy tank top that hugged her breasts and khaki shorts that showcased her stunning legs.

What stuck in his craw was that she was right on one point. It *was* his fault that he had lost this property. If he had wanted it so badly, he should have made a generous offer and sealed the deal. Unfortunately, Drew had been in Dubai at the moment the land came on the market. His business manager, a smart, well-intentioned employee, had taken the initiative and made an offer on Drew's behalf.

No one had imagined that the small farm would attract any buyers, hence the lowball offer. Drew had been as surprised as anyone to hear he'd been outbid.

Beth touched his arm. "Look at that," she said, pointing.

He tried to ignore the spark of heat where her fingers made contact with his skin. But it was immediately replaced by a chilling sensation as he glanced upward. The clouds had settled into an ominous pattern. It looked as if someone had taken a black marker and drawn a line across the sky—parallel to the ground—about halfway between heaven and earth. Below the line everything seemed normal. But in that unusual formation above, menace lurked.

"It's a wall cloud," he said, feeling the hair on his arms stand up. "I saw one as a kid. We have to take shelter. All hell is about to break loose."

As the words left his mouth, two things happened almost simultaneously. Warning sirens far in the distance sounded their eerie wail. And a dark, perfectly-shaped funnel dropped out of the cloud.

Beth gasped. "Oh, God, Drew."

He grabbed her arm. "The storm cellar. Hurry." He didn't bother asking where it was. Everyone in this part of the country had a shelter as close as possible to an exit from their home, so that if things happened in the middle of the night, everyone could make it to safety.

They ran as if all the hounds of hell were after them. He thought about picking her up, but Beth was in great shape, and her long legs ate up the distance. Her house was a quarter of a mile away. If necessary, they could hit the ground and cover their heads, but he had a bad feeling about this storm.

Beth panted, her face red from exertion. "Are we going to make it?"

He glanced over his shoulder, nearly tripping over a root. "It's headed our way...but at an angle. We *have* to make it. Run, Beth. Faster."

The rain hit when they were still a hundred yards from the house. They were drenched to the bone instantly. It was as if some unseen hand had opened a zipper and emptied the sky. Unfortunately, the rain was the least of their worries. A roar in the distance grew louder, the sound chilling in volume.

They vaulted across the remaining distance, their feet barely touching the ground.

In tandem, they yanked at the cellar doors. The furious wind snatched Beth's side out of her hand, flinging it outward.

"Inside," Drew yelled.

Beth took one last look at the monster bearing down on them, her wide-eyed gaze panicked. But she ducked into the cellar immediately. Drew wrestled one door shut, slid partway down the ladder, and dragged the final side with him, ramming home the board that served as an anchor, threading it through two metal plates.

On the bottom was a large handle. He knew what it was for and wished he didn't. If the winds of the tornado were strong enough, the simple cellar doors would be put to the test.

The dark was menacing for a moment, but gradually his eyes adjusted. Tiny cracks let in slivers of daylight. He turned and found Beth huddled against a cinder block wall. "Come sit down," he said, taking one of her hands in his and drawing her toward the two metal folding chairs. Her fingers were icy as she resisted him.

"I don't want to sit. What are we going to do?"

The storm's fury grew louder minute by minute. He had a sick feeling that Beth's property was going to take a direct hit. Given the angle of the storm's path, it was possible that his place was in danger, too. The most he could do was pray. His crew was trained for emergencies. They would protect human life first, but they would also do everything they could to save the horses.

He ran his hands up and down Beth's arms. She was wet and cold and terrified. Not that she voiced the latter. "Take my shirt, Beth. Here." When he wrapped it around her and she didn't protest, he knew she was seriously rattled. "I'm scared, too," he said, with blunt honesty. "But we'll be okay."

The violent tornado mocked him. Debris began hitting the cellar doors. Beth cried out at one particularly loud blow. She stuffed her fist against her mouth. He put his arms around her and tucked her head against his shoulder.

For the first time, he understood the old life-flashing-before-your-eyes thing. It couldn't end like this. But he had no illusions about the security of their shelter. It was old and not very well built.

How ironic that he was trapped with the one woman who evoked such a confusing mix of emotions. Though he knew her to be tough and independent, in his arms she felt fragile and in need of his protection. He held her tightly, drawing comfort from the human contact.

Regrets choked him as he inhaled the scent of her hair. If they were going to die, he should have kissed her first.

Two

Beth clung to Drew unashamedly. He was her anchor in the storm. The very arrogance that irritated her on an almost daily basis was a plus in this situation. Drew said they were going to be okay. She chose to believe him.

Beneath her cheek she felt the steady, reassuring beat of his heart. His bare skin, lightly dusted with hair, was as warm as hers was cool. If anyone had told her twenty-four hours before that she would be standing in a dark room wrapped in Drew Farrell's arms, she would have laughed her head off. Now, she couldn't imagine letting go.

Above their heads, the winds howled and shrieked like banshees delivering a portent of doom. Time slowed down. Perhaps she should have been making contingency plans for what came next, but the only thing that seemed at all real in this horrifying nightmare was Drew's big warm body sheltering hers.

The small space was claustrophobic. It was dank and dark and smelled of raw dirt. But no matter how lacking in ambience, it felt more like a haven than a grave. At least as long as she had Drew. She couldn't bear to think about what it would have been like to survive this storm alone. For one thing, she wasn't sure she could have closed the cellar doors by herself given the strength of the winds.

How long did a tornado last?

The sound began to fill her head. Just when she thought it couldn't get any louder, it did. She was stunned when Drew released her. He shouted something at her. It took him three tries to make her understand.

"The hinges," he yelled. "They're old. I don't think they're going to hold. Put your arms around my waist and hang on to my belt." She stumbled toward him as he grabbed the handle on the base of the cellar doors and prepared to battle the mighty winds. The thought of Drew getting sucked away from her was more terrifying than the tornado itself. She flung herself against his back, circling his waist with her arms and wrapping her fingers around his belt.

She could actually feel the winds pulling at him. Closing her eyes, she prayed.

Drew was not going to let this son of a bitch win. He'd deal with whatever aftermath they had to sift through. But he and Beth were going to make it. The vicious noise was no longer merely above them. It raged and swelled and battered itself into their small shelter. Beth pressed against him, adding her weight to his.

His fingers were numb already. His grip on the handle weakened as his arms strained to hold on. The pain in his shoulders radiated through his torso into his gut, leaving him breathless. For a split second, one mighty gust ripped at the fragile barrier, actually lifting his feet a couple of inches off the ground.

Despair shredded his determination. His grip was slipping. Life couldn't end like this. If the storm won they would be sucked into oblivion.

It was Beth who saved him, Beth who shored up his will. Even without speaking, she was with him. Fighting. He focused on the sensation of her warm body wrapped around his. Blocking his mind to the pain, he concentrated on her and only her. She held him like a lover. A woman who never wanted to let go.

An enormous crash sent tiny bits of debris filtering through the cracks above them. He heard Beth cry out. The fury of the wind was terrifying. Like some apocalyptic beast locked in struggle with a foe, the tornado did its mad dance.

In a second wave of terror, hail pelted their hiding place. The sound echoed like a million gunshots. He couldn't have heard Beth's voice now even if she *tried* to speak. Pieces of ice big enough to make such a racket would decimate her crops and ruin roofs and property.

The storm crescendoed for long, agonizing minutes. Hail changed to the steadier, quieter deluge of rain. And then it was over. The pressure on the cellar door vanished abruptly, causing him to stagger.

Beth's finger's dug into his waist. In the growing silence as the storm moved away, he could hear her rapid breathing. His own pulse racketed at an alarming rate, helped along by the surge of adrenaline that had stayed with him when he needed it.

He flexed his fingers, forcing them to uncurl. Dropping his arms to his sides, he groaned. "Are you okay?"

He had to *make* her release him. Holding her shoulders, he shook her gently. "It's over, Beth. We made it."

For some reason, it was darker now. Virtually no light found its way into their bolt-hole. He could barely make out her face. "We have supplies," she said, her voice shaky but clear. "I saw a metal box on the floor when we climbed down."

Releasing her reluctantly, he felt around in the darkness until he found the chest. It wasn't locked. Lifting the lid, he located flashlights and handed her one. The illumination they provided enabled him to see her expression. She appeared stunned, perhaps in shock. He didn't feel too steady, himself, for that matter.

Grabbing a couple of water bottles, he pulled her toward the chairs and sat beside her. "Take a minute," he said. "Breathe."

"How do we know it's safe to go out? What if there's another one?"

"I'll check the radar." He pulled his phone from his pocket, touched a couple of icons, and cursed.

"What's wrong?"

"The cell towers must be out. No service at all. We'll give it a few minutes and then see what things are like up top. If we hear the sirens again, we can always come back down here."

"What time is it?"

It was oddly surreal to be asked that question. He honestly had no idea how long they had been in the cellar. It felt like hours. When he checked the illuminated dial of his watch, he shook his head. "It's only four thirty."

"That can't be right."

"Drink some water. Let's catch our breath." Honest to God, he was in no real hurry to survey the damage. He'd seen enough news footage in the past to know what a monster tornado could do. Tuscaloosa, Alabama, Moore, Oklahoma, small towns in Tennessee. Hopefully, Royal's storm hadn't been that bad.

He wasn't counting on it, though. The winds they had heard and *felt* carried the force of destruction. Which meant lots of structural damage, but hopefully, no loss of life.

Beth set her bottle on the floor. She had barely drained an inch. "I can't stay down here anymore. I want to know what happened."

"You realize this isn't going to be a walk in the park." They stood facing each other. He took her hands in his. "We'll deal with whatever it is. We're neighbors. Neighbors help each other."

"Thank you, Drew." She squeezed his fingers and released them. "I can handle it. But not knowing is worse."

"Fair enough. Let's get out of here."

Surviving a ferocious tornado was the most terrifying experience of Beth's life. Right up until the moment she realized they were trapped in an eight by eight storm cellar. Her skin crawled at the thought of being buried alive.

Drew had managed to remove the piece of wood that served as a locking mechanism for the cellar doors, but they wouldn't budge. Something heavy lay against them. Shining a beam of light on her cell mate, she saw the muscles in his arms and torso flex and strain as he tried to dislodge whatever was blocking their escape route.

She turned off the flashlight despite the false sense of security it afforded. Drew was balanced on a step, the awkward position making his job even harder. "Can I help push?" she asked, proud of the calm she projected. The fact that it was entirely false seemed immaterial.

"I don't know if we can both fit on the step, but sure. It can't hurt."

He extended his arm and helped her balance beside him. Bracing themselves, they shoved in tandem against the unforgiving wood. Beth's foot slipped, and she nearly tumbled backward. "Sorry," she muttered.

Drew beat his fist against the doors. "Damn it, this is pointless. It won't budge. Whatever is up there has us pinned down for good. I'm sorry, Beth."

She could do one of two things—indulge in a full-blown panic attack…or convince Drew that she was a calm, rational, capable woman. "No apologies necessary. I'm sure someone will find us. Eventually." *When the roads are cleared and when at least one person remembers that Drew came to Green Acres this afternoon.* She cleared her throat. "Did you happen to mention to anyone at the ranch that you were coming over here to read me the riot act?" *Please say yes, please say yes, please say yes.*

"No." He helped her down to the floor and began to pace. It wasn't much of an exercise since his long legs ate up the space in two strides. "Will your family check up on you?"

"We're not close," she said, choosing not to go into detail. No need for him to see the seedy underbelly of her upbringing. Despite Drew's cell phone experience, she pulled hers out of the pocket of her shorts and tried to make a call. No bars...not even one.

Drew saw what she was doing. "Try a text," he said. "Sometimes those will go through even with no signal."

She stared at the screen glumly, holding up the phone so he could see. "It says *not delivered.*"

"Well, hell."

Her sentiments exactly. "I wish I had eaten lunch."

"Concentrate on something else," he urged. "We don't want to dig into the food supply unless it's absolutely necessary."

What he *wasn't* saying was that they could be trapped for days.

Beth refused to contemplate the implications. The storm cellar was equipped with a small, portable hospital commode tucked in the far corner. Things would have to get pretty bad before she could imagine using the john in front of Drew Farrell. *Oh, Lordy.*

Now all she could think about was waterfalls and babbling brooks and the state of her bladder.

Drew sat down beside her. They had both extinguished their flashlights to save the batteries. She gazed at her phone, feeling its solid weight in her hand as a lifeline. "I suppose we should turn these off."

"Yeah. We need to preserve as much charge as we can. We'll check one or the other on the hour in case service is restored."

"But you don't think it's likely."

"No."

In the semidarkness, soon to get even more inky black when the sun went down, she couldn't see much of him at all. But their chairs were close. She was certain she could feel the heat radiating from his body. "I feel so helpless," she said, unable to mask the quiver in her voice.

"So do I." The tone in his voice was weary, but resigned. It must be unusual for a man who was the undisputed boss of his domain to be bested by an act of nature.

"At least we know someone at the ranch will realize you're missing," she said. "You're an important man."

"I don't know about that, but my brother, Jed, is visiting from Dallas. He'll be looking for me."

She wanted to touch him, to feel that tangible reassurance that she was not alone. But she and Drew did not have that kind of relationship. Even without the filter of social convention, they were simply two people trapped in an untenable situation.

His voice rumbled in her ear. "Why don't we call a truce? Until we get rescued. I've lost the urge to yell at you for the moment."

"Please don't be nice to me now," she begged, her anxiety level rising.

"Why not?"

"Because it means you think we're going to die entombed in the ground."

He shifted on his chair, making the metal creak. "Of course we're not going to die. At the very worst we might have to spend a week or more in here. In which case we'd run out of food and water. We'd be miserable, but we wouldn't die."

"Don't sugarcoat it, Farrell." His analytical summation of their predicament was in no way reassuring.

The dark began to close in on her. Even with Drew at her side, her stomach jumped and pitched with nerves. "I need a distraction," she blurted out. "Tell me an embarrassing story about your past that no one knows."

"That sounds dangerous."

"Not at all. What happens in the storm cellar stays in the storm cellar. You can trust me."

His muffled snort of laughter comforted her in some odd way. She enjoyed this softer side of him. When he stood to pace again, she missed his closeness. His scent clung to the shirt he had given her, so she pulled it more tightly around her in the absence of its owner and waited for him to speak.

Drew was worried. Really worried. Not about his and Beth's situation. He'd leveled with her on that score. But what had his stomach in knots was the bigger picture. He should be out there helping with recovery efforts. To sit idly by—while who knows what tragedy unfolded in Royal and the surrounding environs—made him antsy. He was not a man accustomed to waiting.

He made things happen. *He* controlled his destiny. It was humbling to realize that one random roll of the dice, weather-wise, had completely upended his natural behavior. All he could do at the moment was to reassure Beth and to make sure she was okay. Not that he regarded such responsibility as insignificant. He felt a visceral need to protect her. But he also realized that Beth was a strong woman. If they ever got out of here, she would be right by his side helping where she could. He knew her at least that well.

Her random request was not a bad way to pass the time. He cast back through his memories, knowing there was at least one painful spot worth sharing. The anonymity of the dark made it seem easier.

"I was engaged once," he said.

"Good grief, Drew. I know that. Everyone knows that."

"Okay. Then how about the time I took my dad's car out for a joyride when I was ten years old, smoked a cigar and got sick all over his cream leather upholstery?"

"And you lived to tell the tale?"

"Nobody ever knew. My brother helped me clean up the mess, and I put the car back in its spot before Mom and Dad woke up."

"Are your parents still living?"

"Yes. Why?" he asked, suddenly suspicious. "Are you going to complain to them about their hard-assed son?"

"Don't tempt me. And for the record, my secret is not nearly as colorful. One day when I was nine years old I took money out of my mother's billfold and bought a loaf of bread so I could fix lunch to take to school."

"Seriously?" he asked, wondering if she was deliberately trying to tug at his heartstrings.

Without answering, she stood and went to the ladder, peering up at their prison door. "I don't hear anything at all," she said. "What if we have to spend the night here? I don't want to sleep on the concrete floor. And I'm hungry, dammit."

He heard the moment she cracked. Her quiet sobs raked him with guilt. He'd upset her with his snide comment, and now he had to fix things. Jumping to his feet, he took her in his arms and shushed her. "I'm sorry. I was being a jerk. Tell me the rest."

"No. I don't want to. All I want is to get out of this stupid hole in the ground." Residual fear and tension made her implode.

He let her cry it out, surmising that the tears were healthy. This afternoon had been scary as hell, and to make things worse, they had no clue if help was on the way and no means of communication.

Beth felt good in his arms. Though he usually had the urge to argue with her, this was better. Her hair was still wet, the natural curls alive and thick with vitality. Though he had felt the pull of sexual attraction between them before, he had never acted on it. Now, trapped in the dark with nothing to do, he wondered what would happen if he kissed her.

Wondering led to fantasizing which led to action. Tangling his fingers in the hair at her nape, he tugged back her head and looked at her, wishing he could see her expression. "Better now?" The crying was over except for the occasional hitching breath.

"Yes." He felt her nod.

"I want to kiss you, Beth. But you can say no."

She lifted her shoulders and let them fall. "You saved my life. I suppose a kiss is in order."

He frowned. "We saved *each other's* lives," he said firmly. "I'm not interested in kisses as legal tender."

"Oh, just do it," she said, the words sharp instead of romantic. "We've both thought about this over the last two years. Don't deny it."

He brushed the pad of his thumb over her lower lip. "I wasn't planning to."

When their lips touched, something spectacular happened. Not the pageantry and flourish of fireworks, but something sweeter, softer, infinitely more beautiful. Time stood still. Not as it had in the frantic fury of the storm, but with a hushed anticipation that made him hard as his heart bounced in his chest.

Beth put her arms around his neck and kissed him back. Never in his wildest dreams had he imagined connecting with her at this level in the midst of a dark, dismal, cellar. Women deserved soft sheets and candlelight and sophisticated wooing.

There was, however, something to be said for primeval bonding in life-and-death situations. He was so damned glad he had been with her. In truth, he didn't know if she could have managed to lock herself in the cellar on her own. And if the hinges hadn't held.... It made him ill to think of what might have happened to her.

"Beth?"

"Hmm?" The tone in her voice made him hungry for something that was definitely not on the menu at this moment.

"We need to stop."

"Why? I enjoy kissing you. Who knew?"

He swallowed against a tight throat. "You're doing something to me that won't be entirely comfortable given our situation." Gently pushing his hips against hers, he let her feel the extent of his arousal.

Beth jerked out of his arms so quickly it was a wonder they didn't both end up on the floor. Her voice escalated an octave. "You don't even like me."

Three

Beth was mortified...and aroused...and exhausted from their ordeal. And aroused. Did she say that out loud? Fantasizing about kissing Drew Farrell was nothing like the real deal. For one thing, he was far gentler with her than she'd imagined he'd be. Almost as if he expected her to be afraid of him. Fat chance. She'd been dreaming about this moment for months.

But why did it have to happen in such incredibly drab and dreadful surroundings? As truly thankful and grateful as she was to be alive, getting out of this cheerless hole was fast becoming a necessity. She was pretty tough. Not only that, she had beaten some pretty tough odds to make it as far in life as she had. But claustrophobia and fear of the dark were gaining the upper hand. Even hanky-panky with Drew was not quite enough to steady her nerves when she felt the walls closing in.

She decided to ignore his *situation*. He'd been right to call a halt to their exploratory madness. Such impulsive actions would only embarrass them both after they were rescued.

When she sat down again, her legs weak, Drew resumed his pacing. If sexual energy had an aura, she was pretty sure the two of them could have lit up their confined cell without ever using a flashlight.

Silence reigned after that. With her phone turned off, she had no way to check the time. She didn't want to ask Drew. So she sat.

The chair grew harder. The air grew damper. Far in the distance, she thought she heard the wail of sirens. Not another tornado alarm, but a medical vehicle this time. Now, she could no longer pretend that she and Drew were a couple enjoying an innocent kiss. What waited for them above was terrifying. She had no clue what to expect, and she was pretty sure she didn't want to know.

After a half hour passed in dead quiet, she heard him sigh heavily. He reclaimed his spot beside her, scooting his chair a few inches away from hers. She didn't waste time being offended. It was survival of the fittest at this moment. Sexual insanity would only exacerbate matters.

When he finally spoke, she jumped.

"Did you really steal money to buy bread?"

Drew wasn't sure why he wanted to know. But he did.

After a very long pause, Beth finally spoke. "Yes. My mother was not very responsible when it came to things like that. I often had to fake her signature on permission slips for my brother and me. Most kids learn to count money in kindergarten and first grade because it's part of the curriculum. I learned out of necessity."

Drew sat in silence absorbing the spare details of Beth's story. Contrasting her early life with the way he had grown up made him wince at his good fortune.

He knew instinctively that she wouldn't want his sympathy. So instead, he focused on that kiss. Beth had been eager and responsive and fully in the moment. He adjusted his jeans, groaning inwardly. The last thing he needed right now was to acknowledge an attraction that had been growing for two years. Beth was beautiful and smart and capable. Of course, he was drawn to her. But that didn't mean he had to be stupid. His sole focus at the moment needed to be making sure he and Beth could manage until help arrived.

Her quiet voice startled him. "Will you check the time, please? And see if cell service is back up."

"Sure." He hit the dial on his watch. "Nine o'clock." He turned on his phone, waited, and winced when he saw the battery at sixty-eight percent. "Still nothing."

Sitting was no longer an option. His muscles twitched with the need to do something…anything. He went to the cellar doors and tried again to push upward. Whatever was holding them in place might as well have been an elephant. He and Beth were never going to be able to get out on their own.

Leaning his hip against the ladder, he admitted the truth. "We might as well accept the fact that we're going to be here overnight. It's dark up top. There are probably power lines down and roads that are blocked. Search and rescue will have a wide area to cover, and they may not get to us until morning."

"If then."

He let that one pass. "I think it's time to eat something." Rummaging in the footlocker, he found a small metal tin full of beef jerky. He removed a couple pieces and handed one to Beth. *"Bon appétit."*

She didn't say anything, but he heard the rustle of plastic packaging as she opened the snack.

There were two more box-shaped flashlights in the footlocker. If he wanted to, he could turn on one of the smaller ones they were already using to illuminate their living space—until the juice ran out. But on the off chance their incarceration lasted longer than twenty-four hours or more, it made sense to preserve the batteries.

He rummaged a second time and handed Beth a bottle of water. "Drink only half if you can. We need to hope for the best and plan for the worst."

"If we ever get out of here, I'll put that on a T-shirt for you. *The wisdom of Drew Farrell.*"

"Are you making fun of me?"

"Not at all. Merely trying to stave off feminine hysteria."

He grinned in the darkness, chewing the jerky and swallowing it with a grimace. "You're about the least hysterical woman I've ever met."

"I have my moments."

"Not that I've seen. I admire you, Beth, despite my grousing."

"There you go again…being nice. It creeps me out."

"That's because you've only seen one side of me. I can actually be quite a gentleman when I choose. Case in point, I promise not to have my wicked way with you while we sleep tonight."

She laughed out loud. "I don't think I can get down on this floor unless we turn on a light and check for spiders and other nasty stuff."

The husky feminine amusement in her voice made him happy. At least he'd distracted her for a moment. "That's doable. I came across one of those reflective silver space blankets in the trunk. I thought we could spread that on the ground. It won't make us any more comfortable, but at least it will be clean. I'll sit up and lean against the wall. You can put your head in my lap for a pillow."

"You can't sleep sitting up. Either we both lie down, or we perch on these folding chairs until we fall over."

"Stubborn woman."

"Definitely the pot calling the kettle black."

"Are you tired?"

"I don't really know. All my synapses are fried. Sheer terror will do that to you."

She was right. The adrenaline had flowed hot and heavy this afternoon. "I'm betting if we keep still long enough we might be able to sleep. We'll need rest to handle whatever happens tomorrow."

He heard rather than saw her stand up. When her hand touched his arm, he realized that she had come to him.... one human seeking comfort from another. "It's going to be bad, isn't it?"

He nodded, squeezing her hand briefly. "Yeah. Wind strong enough to lift whatever is on top of us will have done a hell of a lot of damage."

Her sigh was audible. "Let's get settled for the night, then. The sooner we sleep, the sooner morning will come."

Beth wanted to weep with joy when Drew turned on one of the flashlights so they could construct their makeshift bed. Being able to see his face gave her a shot of confidence and relief. Everything in Royal might have changed, but Drew was still Drew. His features were drawn and tired, though. She could only imagine what *she* looked like. It was probably a good thing she didn't have a mirror. Her hair felt like a rat's nest.

Thankfully, the cellar was not as bad as she'd imagined. Drew checked every corner and cranny, killing a couple of spiders, but nothing major. By the time they had spread the silver blanket on the floor, she was more than ready to close her eyes.

But first, she had to deal with something that couldn't wait. "Drew...I...." Her face flamed.

He was quick on the uptake. "We'll both use the facilities." He went to the ladder and stood with his back to her, beaming the flashlight toward the cellar doors, diffusing the illumination so that she could see but not feel exposed.

Beth did what had to be done and swapped places with him. In hindsight, it was not nearly as embarrassing as she had expected. She and Drew were survivors in a bad situation. No point in being prissy or overly modest.

At last, they were ready to court sleep. She knelt awkwardly, wincing when the concrete floor abraded her knees through the thin barrier that was their only comfort. She curled onto her side, facing the wall.

Drew joined her, facing the same direction, but leaving a safe distance between them. "All set?" he asked.

"Yes. But I should give you your shirt. You'll get cold."

"I'm fine." He sighed, a deep, ragged exhale that could have meant anything. "I'm turning off the light now."

Her stomach clenched. "Okay."

This time the darkness was even worse after she'd been able to see for the last half hour. Her eyes stung with tears she would not let fall. She was okay. Drew was okay. That was all that mattered.

Her heart thundered too rapidly for sleep. And she couldn't regulate her breathing. She trembled all over— delayed reaction probably.

Drew's arms came around her, dragging her against him, his hands settling below her breasts. "Relax, Beth. Things will look better in the morning."

The feel of his warm chest against her back kept her sane—that and his careful embrace. Her head rested on his arm. It must have been painful for him, but he didn't voice a single complaint.

"Thank you," she whispered.

"Go to sleep."

For Drew, the night was a million hours long. He barely slept—and then only in snatches. His gritty eyes and aching body reminded him that he wasn't a kid anymore. But even a teenager would have trouble relaxing on a bare cement floor. To take his mind off the physical discomfort, he concentrated on Beth.

It took her a half hour to fall asleep. He knew, because he kept sneaking peeks at his watch. Her body had been tense in his embrace, either from the miserable sleeping arrangements, or because she was uneasy about their inescapable physical intimacy. Or perhaps both.

Either way, she finally succumbed to exhaustion.

He liked holding her. As he tucked a swath of hair behind her ear, he inhaled the faint scent of her shampoo. Apple maybe…or some other fruity smell. In the dark, his senses were magnified. The curl he wrapped around his finger was soft and springy and damp. He allowed himself for one indulgent moment to imagine Beth's beautiful hair tumbling across his chest as they made love.

The image took his breath away. All these months of verbal sparring had hidden a disturbing truth. He was hungry for Beth Andrews—totally captivated by her spunky charm—and physically drawn to her sexy body.

If he hadn't been in pain, and if every one of his muscles weren't drained from battling a tornado, he would have been more than a little aroused. As it was, his body reacted. But only for a short moment. He closed his eyes and prayed for oblivion.

Beth woke up with a sensation of doom she couldn't shake. It was only after she opened her eyes that she remembered why. Her concrete prison was still intact with no way out.

Despite the circumstances, it wasn't the worst *morning after* she'd ever experienced. Far from it. Drew's right arm lay heavy across her waist. His right hand cupped her breast. Even though his gentle snore reassured her that he was still asleep, she blushed from her toes to her hairline. Until yesterday, Drew Farrell had been nothing more than her annoying, arrogant neighbor.

Except for the fact that he was incredibly gorgeous, masculine and sexy, she had been able to ignore him and his continuing dissatisfaction with her thriving business. But now, in one brief stormy adventure, they had been thrust together in a pressure cooker. No longer were they merely bickering acquaintances.

For better or for worse, they were comrades in arms. Friends.

It was difficult to sleep with someone, even fully clothed, and not experience a sense of intimacy. Not necessarily sexual intimacy, though that was certainly a real possibility when it came to her feelings for Drew.

But they shared another equally real type of closeness. They had stared death in the face.

Even now the words sounded too dramatic. But when she remembered looking over her shoulder and seeing the monster storm barreling toward them with ferocity, something inside her shivered with dread. Disaster had come close enough to breathe down their necks. They had escaped with their lives, but they weren't out of the woods yet.

It was probably still early. Whatever landed on them during the tornado had darkened most of the tiny holes in the cellar doors that let in light. But the few that were left filtered the faint glow of dawn.

She felt no real urgency to move. Though her hip ached where it had spent the better part of the night battling with the unforgiving floor, she was surprisingly content. Being held close in Drew's warm, comforting embrace was better than a tranquilizer. His big body was hard and muscular, reminding her without words that she was under the protection of a confident, capable male.

There was something to be said for primitive responses. Though Beth could hold her own in most situations, the fact remained that Drew was larger and stronger and more equipped to deal with the physical challenges of their crisis.

She let her mind wander. How badly had her farm been damaged? What about Drew's horses? And the town of Royal? Had it avoided a direct hit? Thankfully, the storm had struck late enough in the day that most children would have already been home from school. But businesses in town would still have been open.

The not knowing drove her crazy. Even so, worrying accomplished nothing. She had no other choice but to live in the moment.

Closing her eyes, she savored the unfamiliar sensation of her cheek resting on Drew's arm. The light covering of masculine hair tickled her nose. His scent was so familiar to her now that she could pick him out of a crowd in a dark room.

He must be very uncomfortable. But there was no reason to wake him. Had he thought it odd to hold her like this?

They had been adversaries from the beginning. It seemed he was always rubbing his good fortune in her face. Though perhaps she was too sensitive on that score, because most people thought he was a great guy. In fact, the only person she knew in Maverick County who ever got crossways with the owner of Willowbrook Farms was Beth Andrews.

Their feud had gone on a long time, probably because they were too much alike. Both stubborn. Both sure they were right.

He muttered in his sleep, tightening his grasp, his fingers brushing her nipple though three thin layers: his shirt, her tank top, and a lacy bra. Was he dreaming about a woman?

Unbidden, arousal stirred in Beth's veins. It was sweet and yearning and ultimately for naught. Nothing was going to happen. The time and place were wrong. More importantly, she and Drew had to hope that rescue was on the way and that whatever they discovered above ground was not going to be too terrible.

She felt his steady breathing ruffle the hair at her nape. Had he thought about kissing her there? Or had he been too wiped out to even notice she was a woman? How sad that their first opportunity to really get to know each other was fraught with difficulty and struggle.

Being Drew's neighbor had been a pain in the ass until today. His repeated bluster about the problems her business caused his had added to the stress of getting the farm up and running. In the midst of his frequent complaints, she had been busy tending to her fledgling crops, learning new things she needed to know and trying to keep the checkbook in the black.

Now, there would be no going back. What would this new awareness mean to their ongoing battle?

Sometime later she realized that she must have dozed off again. One of her legs was trapped between Drew's thighs. It was as if his body was trying to stake a claim. She knew she should wake him, if only to let him move his arm. But this moment was pleasurable despite the context.

Once they were officially awake and alert, they would have to face things like a tiny water supply, dwindling stores of food, and the reality that no one knew where they were. All the harsh realities that defined them at the moment.

Given that truth, she closed her eyes and drifted back to sleep.

* * *

When Drew woke up, he stifled a groan. His body was one big throbbing toothache, and he wasn't at all sure he would be able to stand. But having Beth tucked up against him was a bonus. Carefully, he eased his arm out from under her head, wincing as the blood returned. Beth muttered and frowned when her cheek came to rest on the unsympathetic ground.

He checked his watch. Seven thirty. Surely late enough for police and rescue personnel to begin going house to house. Rolling to his feet, he tried to ignore the sudden craving for eggs and bacon and hot coffee. Sadly, beef jerky was on the menu again. But not until Beth joined him.

Standing on the ladder, he turned on his phone and held it as close as he could to the cellar doors, praying for a signal. Still nothing…not that he really expected an overnight miracle. The storm had probably destroyed numerous cell towers.

He heard Beth sit up. "Any change?" she asked.

He wanted to be able to give her good news, but there was none. "No. You okay?" She was nothing more than a dim outline in the gloom.

"I've been better."

"We have to eat and drink something. If this drags on, we'll need to keep our energy up." He hopped down from his perch and located more beef jerky and water. "Welcome to breakfast, *Survivor*-style."

"Thanks. I think."

He joined her on the floor, their knees touching as they sat cross-legged on the crinkly blanket. "Somehow, during all those years in the Boy Scouts, I never imagined this scenario."

"Did you make it all the way to Eagle?"

"Yeah. My dad was a stickler for never giving up on anything."

"Ah, now I get it," she said. "That's why you continue to browbeat me."

"Eat your breakfast, woman."

If he had to be trapped in a hole in the ground, Beth was the perfect companion. She hadn't whined. She hadn't panicked. Her sense of humor had survived the tornado intact even though she had to know, as he did, that things would probably get worse before they got better.

Holding her as they slept last night tapped into more than his human need to cheat death. With all the societal expectations stripped away, he discovered something deeper than physical attraction. Beth Andrews had edged her way into his heart.

That information was sensitive—need-to-know basis only. But it was something to be tucked away and savored at a later date.

"Seriously, Drew. What are we going to do to pass the time? If we can't use our flashlights, our options are seriously limited."

Several inappropriate suggestions came to mind immediately. But he squelched the impulse to voice them. "We can try lifting the doors again."

"And that will take all of ten minutes."

"Sarcasm, Beth? I thought we'd reached a détente."

A faint noise from above interrupted her answer. He put a hand on her knee. "Shh...did you hear that?"

Four

They both froze, their ears straining in the darkness. Next came the screech of metal, followed by a muffled shout. "Anybody down there?"

Drew leapt to his feet, dragging Beth with him. "Yes," he shouted. "Yes."

Beth was trembling. Hell, he probably was, too. He wrapped his arm around her narrow waist and she curled her arms around him. Together, they faced the specter of uncertainty.

They waited for what seemed like forever but might only have been a minute or two. Thumps and curses rained down on them, along with dust particles that made them cough. The voice came again, louder this time. "Hang on."

Beth leaned into him. "What's taking so long?"

"I think they're trying to move whatever has the doors stuck. It must be big."

She murmured something under her breath.

"What?" he asked, still straining to hear what was going on up top.

"I hope the doors don't break and whatever that is doesn't fall and crush us in this pit."

He chuckled, despite the tension gripping him. "An active imagination can be a curse at times."

"Tell me about it."

They fell silent again. All the commotion above them had ceased. Surely the rescue team had heard him shout.

Beth voiced his concern. "What if they didn't hear you? What if they went away?"

"I don't think they would give up without making sure no one is down here...even if they *didn't* hear me."

But doubt began to creep in. Why was nothing happening?

Beth burrowed her face into his chest. He held her close. "Don't freak out. If they left, they'll come back." *God, I hope so.*

He checked his watch. "It's almost nine."

"What time did we hear the first shout?" The words were muffled.

"I'm not sure. Maybe ten minutes ago? Fifteen?"

The return of absolute silence was infinitely more difficult than if they had never received a ray of hope.

Beth was shaking.

He rubbed her back. "Hang on. We've made it this far."

Suddenly, the loud racket returned, a shrill high-pitched noise that might have been a winch. Then a dreadful dragging scrape, and finally a human shout.

Seconds later the cellar doors were flung wide. The brilliant sunlight, after hours of captivity, blinded them.

A figure crouched at the opening. "Ms. Andrews? Are you down there?"

Drew shielded his eyes with his arm. "She is. And me, too. Is that you, Jed?"

The minutes that followed were chaos. Drew boosted Beth up the ladder, passing her up to helping hands, and then followed her. He grabbed his brother in a bear hug. "God, I'm so glad to see you."

Jed's face was grim. "You scared the hell out of me. No one had any idea where you were." Two EMTs muscled in, checking Drew's and Beth's blood pressure, firing off questions, taking care of business. Drew gave a terse summation of the events that had stranded them below ground.

It was easy to see why he and Beth had been trapped. Her small car, now a mangled mess of metal, had been snatched up and dumped…right on top of the cellar.

When the immediate furor died, he searched for Beth. She had walked several hundred feet away and stood gazing at what was left of her fall pumpkin crop. Virtually nothing. The tornado had ripped across her land, decimating everything in its path.

The front left portion of her bungalow was sheared off, but two-thirds of the house remained intact.

He stood by her side. "I'll help you with repairs."

She turned to face him, her expression lost. "I appreciate the offer. But unless you know how to grow a pumpkin overnight, my revenue stream just vanished until June at the earliest." She searched his face. "What did he tell you about *your* place?"

The day was already heating up. Beth slipped off his shirt and handed it to him. He slid his arms into it and fastened a few buttons. "I was very lucky. We lost a lot of fencing…and one outbuilding. But the staff and the horses are all safe."

"Your house?"

"Minor stuff."

Jed joined them. "Let's get you two back to Willowbrook. You can shower and have a decent meal."

Beth glanced at Drew's brother, her eyes haunted. "Tell us about Royal. How bad is it?"

Jed hesitated.

Drew squeezed Beth's hand. "Tell us, Jed. We've been imagining the worst."

Jed's shoulders slumped. He bent his head and stared

at the ground before looking up with a grim-faced stare. "Mass destruction. The storm was an EF4. A quarter-mile wide and on the ground for twenty-two miles. The center of the storm missed Willowbrook, but it turned and traveled straight over Beth's place and on east."

"God help us," Drew said. Nothing so tragic had ever touched the town of Royal. "How many dead?"

"As of this morning, the count stood at thirteen. A family of four…tourists. They took shelter beneath an overpass, but you know how dangerous that is. A young couple in a mobile home."

Beth put her hand to her mouth, tears spilling down her cheeks. "And the other seven?"

Jed's jaw worked as if couldn't form the words. "The town hall was destroyed."

"Jesus." Drew's stomach pitched. Beth sobbed openly now.

Jed shook his head, grief on his face. "The deputy mayor is dead. Also, Craig Richardson, who owned the Double R. Plus five others who were in the building at the time."

"And the mayor? Richard Vance?" Drew knew the man by sight and respected him.

"Life threatening injuries. But stable. I don't have a clue about the total number injured. The hospital is overloaded but managing."

Beth put her hand on Jed's arm briefly, claiming his attention. "A pregnant woman. She stopped by my produce stand just before the storm hit. Do you know anything about her?"

"I'm afraid I do. We found her car late last night when we were searching for the two of you. The tornado flipped her vehicle. She has severe head injuries, so they've put her in a medically induced coma."

Beth had stopped crying and now visibly pulled herself together. "And the baby?"

"Delivered by emergency C-section. Last I heard, they think she will make it."

Drew remembered the odd feeling that he knew the woman. "Do you know the mother's name?"

"They've listed her for now as a *Jane Doe*. Her car was destroyed. Cell phone and purse missing, probably in someone's backyard five miles away."

Jed motioned toward his car. "We need to go. Drew, after you've had a few minutes to rest, I know they could use the two of us in town."

Beth still stared at her forlorn house. "You guys go on. I'll stay here. There's plenty to do."

Drew realized then that Beth was definitely in shock. He put his arm around her shoulders, steering her toward the car. It disturbed him that her skin was icy cold. "We can bring some tarps over this evening, but you can't stay here. I know you don't want to enter the enemy camp, but I'll promise you good food, a hot shower and a bed for as long as you need it."

Beth allowed Drew to take charge because it was in her best interests and because she was too disheartened to deal with anything but basic needs at the moment.

The road between her house and the magnificent entrance to Willowbrook Farms was two miles long. Ninety-nine percent of the time when Beth departed her property, she turned left out of her driveway. So it felt odd to be deliberately closing the gap between her home and Drew's. She had only been out this way once or twice, more out of curiosity than anything else. Both times she had been struck by the pristine appearance of Drew's ranch. It was an enormous, well-cared-for equine operation.

As they drove along—slowly because of the debris littering the road—it was far too easy to see the storm's path. The twister had clipped a section of Drew's acreage, veered toward the private road and traveled along it until deciding to thunder across Beth's once thriving farm. She knew in her heart she was lucky her house was still standing. There were almost surely others in far more dire straits.

"I should have gotten clean clothes," she cried, realizing her omission.

Drew shook his head vehemently. "You can't go inside your house until an expert checks for structural damage. Not unless you want to chance spending another night beneath a pile of rubble."

"Low blow, Farrell," she muttered. "What am I supposed to wear? I have plans to burn this current outfit."

"I have seven women on my staff. I'm sure between them they can come up with a solution."

By the time they finally pulled up in front of Drew's classic two-story farmhouse, she was so tired her eyes had trouble focusing. He helped her out of the car. Jed followed them inside.

Drew took her arm, steering her toward the back of the house. "Food first."

"And a bathroom."

That made him grin. "Of course."

Jed smiled as well. "If you would like me to, while the two of you are eating, I can round up some necessities for Ms. Andrews and have the housekeeper put them in a guest room."

"That would be wonderful. Thank you. And please call me Beth. I'm pretty sure that rescuing me from a storm cellar puts us on a first name basis."

She was surprised when Drew spoke up, his face a mix of emotions. "Thanks, Jed. That would be great. Get a couple of the women in the front office to help you. But I'll pick out a bedroom."

The brothers exchanged an odd glance that Beth was unable to decipher.

In the kitchen, the housekeeper was waiting. Evidently, she had been on standby since Jed called to say he thought Drew and Beth had been found.

The size of the breakfast was overwhelming, but Beth did her best to try some of everything. Biscuits, ham, fresh peaches and eggs so light and fluffy they almost floated off the plate. Beth hated eating in her grubby clothes, but her stomach held sway, demanding to be fed. The coffee was something exotic and imported. Nothing at all like the stuff she drank at home.

She and Drew exchanged barely a dozen words as they ate. The housekeeper had excused herself, leaving them to their meal in private. Surrounded by windows, the cozy breakfast nook overlooked a small pond.

Drew touched the back of her hand briefly. "Promise me you'll take a nap. You've been through a lot in the last twenty-four hours."

Her eyes teared up again. She hated feeling so emotional, but the enormity of what had happened was almost impossible to comprehend. And she hadn't even seen the damage elsewhere.

"You were right there with me. How can Jed expect you to go into town when you're exhausted?"

"I'll be fine. My house wasn't torn apart. You've had a terrible shock. Give yourself time to get back on your feet."

"I'll nap," she said, knowing that he was right. "But after that I want to do something to help out in the community."

His bright blue eyes warmed her to the bone. "Fair

enough. And I swear to you that we'll take care of securing your house before dark."

"Thanks." She felt shy suddenly, sitting beside him in this brightly lit room. All of the appliances looked like something out of a catalog. Compared to her small, antiquated kitchen, this room was worthy of a palace.

That impression only increased as Drew ushered her down a hallway and into a large guest suite. Throughout the house, she saw beautiful, gleaming hardwood floors, accented by Oriental rugs that were probably more expensive than her car. Or what used to be her car. Panic encroached as she contemplated everything she needed to do in the aftermath of the storm. In addition to handling details about insurance claims and repairs, she wasn't sure she had enough cash flow to wait for checks to arrive.

Drew interrupted her internal meltdown. "I thought you would like this side of the house. It gets the morning sun and you can spot the last of the hummingbirds stopping by our feeders on the way south."

He stood with his hands in his pockets as if he didn't know what to do with them. His obvious unease was so unusual she was taken aback. "Something's bothering you," she said quietly.

"Not bothering me," he said quickly. "But I do have something important I want to say to you."

"What is it?" Her stomach quivered. She couldn't imagine what they had to discuss at this moment.

"I want you to live here at Willowbrook…until the repairs on your house are completed. No hidden agenda, I swear. I know we don't see eye to eye, but we need to table our disagreement in the short term while things are in chaos."

Her stomach fell to her knees. He was entirely serious. Though it seemed he was trying to be nice, suspicion reared its ugly head. "We don't even know each other," she said faintly.

Drew leaned against a post of the giant rice-carved bed and gave her a crooked smile. "I'm not sure you can say that anymore. We've lived a lifetime in the last twenty-four hours, don't you think? I have plenty of room, and you would have online access and fax machines to deal with your insurance claims. You wouldn't have to worry about grocery shopping or cooking or anything else. You could concentrate on getting Green Acres back in shape."

What he offered was infinitely tempting. Her world was in tatters. But she was a mature woman. Would taking Drew's help be too needy?

"I'll think about it," she said. "Thank you for the invitation."

"Accepting help doesn't mean you're weak, Beth."

"What, you're a mind reader now?"

He crossed to where she stood by the window. "I'm grateful that my house is still standing. But if it weren't, I would gladly accept a helping hand from my neighbor."

"Horse hockey," she said, laughing in spite of herself.

"It's true. So please swallow your pride and let me do this for you."

He liked the notion of being her savior. She could tell. It was a guy thing. Looking around the sumptuous, exquisitely decorated bedroom, she grimaced inwardly. This was a far cry from the roach-infested apartments where she had grown up. It was difficult to admit, even to herself, how much she wanted to stay.

On a normal day, she might have summoned the strength to turn him down. But after the tornado and last night's ordeal, she was working from a final store of reserves. "I suppose I'd be a fool to say no."

"I happen to know you're a very smart woman."

She couldn't allow herself to depend on him indefinitely. This gilded world of wealth and privilege was not hers. The life she had carved out for herself was a good one, but it wasn't this.

Even so, surely it couldn't hurt to pretend for a while. "Okay," she sighed. "You win. But only because I'm at a low point. And because I'm guessing that bathroom over there has a jetted tub."

"You are and it does."

Something happened then—something she couldn't explain. The attraction that neither of them had acknowledged over the last months and days was tangible now. Fired in the crucible of the tornado's fury, it had proven to be far more real than she could ever have imagined.

Desire hovered between them...around them. Drew's expression was serious now. His warm gaze seeped into her bones, rejuvenating her. Did his interest in her have an ulterior motive? Did he think if they were intimate, he could manipulate her more easily? "I know what you're thinking," she said.

Hunger flashed in his eyes. "Not the half of it," he muttered.

His mouth settled over hers in slow motion. Their lips met, clung. Strong arms circled her waist, pulling her up against his big, hard frame.

Dimly, in some far recess of her subconscious, she understood that this was a really bad idea. Living in Drew's house...accepting his help. *Playing with fire.*

When his tongue slid between her lips, stroking inside her mouth intimately, a curl of desire, sweet and hot, made her legs tremble. She clung to him, flashing back to their terrifying dash to the storm cellar. Would she have made it in time without him? Awash with emotions that ran the gamut from gratitude to sheer need, she kissed him back.

Drew said she was a smart woman. But here, locked in his arms, with his mouth hot and demanding on hers, she knew that she was not. Despite every obstacle standing in their way, both past and present, she wanted to share his bed.

The town they both loved had been ripped apart. Lives were lost. Her own home was in shambles.

Perhaps it was the very existence of disaster that made her reach for what she wanted. Life was short. Life was precious. Even without a happy ending, she could have Drew. It wasn't vanity to think so. She saw it in his eyes, felt it in the restless caress of his hands.

Deliberately, she nipped his bottom lip with her teeth. "You have things to do. But I'll be here when you're ready."

Five

I'll be here when you're ready. Drew replayed that sentence in his head a thousand times as he made his way from stall to stall checking on his horses. He relied on top-notch employees. But he wanted to see for himself that the horses were safe. These beautiful animals were more than dollar signs to him. They were noble steeds with bloodlines that went further back than his own.

He spoke softly to each one, smiling when a whinny of recognition greeted him. They were muscle and sinew and most of all—heart. Ever since he was a boy, he had loved the sights and sounds and smells of the horse barn. As an adult, he was fortunate to make his living working with these creatures. Though he would be reluctant to admit it, he grieved each time one of his prized stallions left the ranch.

An hour later, walking shoulder to shoulder with Jed down the streets of Royal—or what was left of them—he forgot all about Willowbrook. The random pattern of the destruction was hard to fathom. On one block, houses had been razed to the ground, no more than piles of rubble. But one road over, dwellings were untouched.

The west side of town was hardest hit; almost all of the businesses there a total loss. Smaller tornadoes had touched down across the county.

Drew had seen TV coverage of bad tornadoes. In his lifetime he'd personally witnessed a few storms that ripped up trees and tore off roofs. But nothing like this. Ever. The governor and his entourage had helicoptered in at daybreak and assessed the damage in preparation for a news conference. Faces from national news stations and The Weather Channel popped up everywhere. That, more than anything else, brought home the enormity of the disaster.

Royal was about to become famous for all the wrong reasons.

Earlier in the day, Jed had made contact with the point man for search and rescue. Now, he and Drew and a half dozen other members of the Texas Cattleman's Club joined a team with canine support going from house to house looking for survivors. Thankfully, almost everyone had been accounted for by this point. While Drew and Beth had been trapped in the cellar the afternoon and evening before, the immediate rush to find missing and dead had been urgent and thorough.

Today was about making sure nothing was overlooked. Sometimes the elderly had no one to raise a red flag if they went missing. And they might be too weak to cry out for help. Hence, the careful attention of a half dozen teams working a grid system across the town.

Drew squatted in a sea of pink insulation and crumpled Sheetrock to pick up a lavender teddy bear, probably some little girl's prized possession. He set it in a prominent place, hoping someone would find it.

Families were beginning the grim and heartbreaking task of sifting through what was left of their homes in an effort to reclaim valuables. National Guard units patrolled the hardest hit neighborhoods, discouraging looting.

Royal was a great place to live and raise a family, but

in situations of chaos, the occasional vermin crawled out
to prey on others' misfortune.

By the time the sun hung low in the sky, Drew was beat.
He and Jed grabbed a burger at a restaurant offering free
dinners to rescue personnel. They stood outside to eat, in
full view of what was left of Town Hall. Almost all of the
three-story building had been leveled. Only a portion of
the clock tower still stood, the hands of time perpetually
frozen at 4:14.

Drew's stomach knotted. He tossed the last half of his
meal in a trash receptacle and stared at the eerie scene.
It was painful remembering where he and Beth had been
at the moment they heard the sirens. Why had they been
spared when others had not?

It was one of those questions with no answer.

He turned his back on the tragic scene and rubbed the
heels of his hands over his eyes. Jed's light touch on his
shoulder startled him.

"You doin' okay, big brother?"

Drew nodded automatically, but inside he wondered if
anything would ever be okay again. "Yeah."

Jed rolled his neck. "A bunch of the TCC guys and gals
are going to meet at the club first thing in the morning for
another follow-up meeting."

"Good idea." Jed lived in Dallas and was a part of that
branch of the Texas Cattleman's Club. He was only visiting Royal for the moment, but he knew most of the same
people Jed knew. Unfortunately, he'd picked a hell of a time
to come. Drew was glad to have him around.

"I ran into Gil Addison while you were talking to the
fire chief. Gil has been coordinating the whole thing. He
wants to ensure that we're pooling resources and maxi-
mizing relief efforts."

"Makes sense." Gil owned a thriving ranch south of

town and had been TCC president for two years. Drew checked his watch. "I promised Beth we'd get her house secure before tonight. We'd better head back."

"Suits me. There's going to be plenty to do tomorrow."

Beth couldn't wait to see Drew again. When he wandered into the kitchen, she could see from his expression that the work today had been heartbreaking and difficult.

"Have you eaten?" she asked.

"Jed and I got a burger in town."

"You want some dessert? Mrs. Simmons made apple pie."

"Maybe later. We need to get out to your place."

She nodded. "Your foreman has been so kind. He's already loaded everything we'll need into the back of your truck."

"Jed's going to help me. You don't have to go. It might be dangerous."

She frowned. "It's my house."

"Fine," he said, his tone resigned. "Be out front in five minutes."

Beth grabbed a jacket and a flashlight. Despite what Drew had said that morning, she planned to recover a few valuables. She lived out in the country, but even so, she didn't like the idea of her home being vulnerable to anyone who chose to intrude. Drew was used to being obeyed. That much was clear. But he would have to get over it. Accepting his help did *not* mean letting him boss her around.

He climbed behind the wheel of his huge truck, leaving Beth and Jed to enter from the other side. Beth found herself sandwiched between two handsome Farrell males. Both men carried an air of exhaustion. She decided then and there not to deliberately provoke Drew.

He had been out working, while *she* had enjoyed the

luxury of a wonderful nap tucked beneath a fluffy comforter, resting on sheets soft as a whisper. The bed Drew had chosen for her was huge and comfy and decadent. Did he have any thought of sharing it with his guest at some point in the future?

Her focus changed entirely as they traveled the relatively short distance between the two properties. Not a word was spoken in the cab of the truck as they witnessed the storm's track. It had effectively ripped a trail along the private road, turning abruptly to power over Beth's property and head toward town.

As they parked in front of her house and got out, the memories of the tornado came rushing back. *It's over,* she told herself repeatedly, but still her knees knocked and her stomach pitched.

She touched Drew's arm, her gaze beseeching. "I'd like to get my computer and pack a few clothes. If I go in through the side that's not damaged, I'm sure it will be fine."

He glanced back at Jed. "I'll stay with her. Do you mind sorting out the supplies? We'll do the tarps in a few minutes."

Jed nodded. "No problem."

Beth's house was small, but even so, it was almost unbelievable to see what was damaged and what was not. The back of the house was relatively unscathed. One broken window...a few shingles missing. The bedrooms were habitable. At the front of the house, the small living room wasn't in bad shape except where a piece of lumber had punctured the vinyl siding. But the kitchen was a mess. The tornado had ripped apart one quarter of the house, shattering crockery and literally plucking off the roof and twisting it into an unrecognizable mess.

Standing in what used to be the doorway to her kitchen,

Beth lifted her shoulders and let them fall. "Well," she said, forcing words from a tight throat. "I needed new appliances anyway."

Drew took her hand and tugged her backward to a safer part of the house. "Don't go in there, please. Anything could fall on your head. And Beth...." He trailed off, his expression troubled.

"What?"

"Just because the rest of the home *seems* intact doesn't mean that it is. It's entirely possible that the house was momentarily lifted off its foundation. Which means you may have structural damage that could result in leaks or other problems. I don't want to upset you, but it's better to assume the worst and then be happy if it turns out not to be as bad as we think."

He was right, of course. But hearing it laid out logically did nothing to lessen the impact of what had happened. She had worked so hard for this house. It was more than four walls and a roof. It was a symbol of all she had overcome. Seeing it in shambles broke her heart.

With Drew hovering, she quickly packed a bag with as many clothes as she could grab. Other than her computer and some pieces of jewelry, the only things worth stealing were her television and Blu-ray player. She sincerely doubted anyone would go to the trouble to drive out here and take electronics, so she left the living room as it was. As she handed off her small suitcase to Drew, it occurred to her that theft might be the least of her worries. What was going to happen when it rained? The tarps were surely a short-term solution.

Clearly, she wasn't doing a very good job of hiding her jangled emotions. Drew hugged her with his free arm. "I know it seems overwhelming, but I'll help you get things back together. Contractors, plumbers.... whoever else you need. You do have insurance, right?"

"Yes, thank God. And I think it's pretty good. But I've never had to use it."

"C'mon," he said. "It's almost dark. We have to string up the tarps while we can still see."

They carried her things out to the truck and put them in the jump seat. Jed had already untangled ropes and unfolded three enormous sheets of heavy plastic. Beth leaned against the hood and watched as her Good Samaritans struggled and cursed and finally managed to get the first tarp in place. Gradually they encased the broken portion of the house in a shroud of overlapping layers.

It wasn't airtight. And it wouldn't keep out varmints, animal or otherwise. But hopefully it would protect her personal belongings from the weather. If she had to, she would rent a storage unit and move her things out of the house until the repairs were done. Since most of her furniture was thrift shop in origin, she wasn't too worried.

Darkness closed in on them. As Drew and his brother tied off the last corners and used duct tape to secure vulnerable spots, Beth wandered over to the storm cellar. Squatting, she opened one side of the double doors. Without wind to contend with, it was as easy as raising a window. Nothing was visible down below. But she remembered. She would always remember.

Drew lowered the ladder and shoved it into the bed of the truck. His eyes were on Beth. She seemed so alone, it made his chest hurt.

Jed tossed a canvas bag of supplies on top of the ladder. "So what's the deal with you and Beth Andrews?"

Still watching Beth, Drew shrugged. "We're neighbors. That's all."

"C'mon, Bro. I wasn't born yesterday. This *thing* you two have between you is more than surviving a tornado."

Drew shot his brother a disgusted look. "Have I butted in about you and Kimberly? Drop it, Jed."

"Fair enough. But be careful. Sometimes women mistake kindness for something else. It wouldn't be fair to lead her on."

"One budding relationship in your pocket and suddenly you're an expert. Get over yourself. I can handle my love life without your help."

Jed grinned smugly. "Who said anything about love?"

Muttering under his breath, Drew strode over to where Beth stood looking at the mass of metal and tires that had once been her car. "I've got an old rattletrap of a pickup out at the house," he said. "We use it sometimes to run errands on the ranch. But you're welcome to it for as long as necessary."

Finally, she faced him. "I hate taking charity," she said, her gaze stormy. "I'm already staying in your house. This is too much."

"What does it matter, Beth? It's not your fault the tornado struck here. It's a whim of fate or whatever you want to call it." He felt guilty that his place had been mostly spared. He would do whatever he could to help rebuild Royal. And he would start with Beth's little bungalow.

It was so dark now he could barely see her face. "Let's go." She allowed him to take her arm and steer her toward the truck, but he knew she was struggling to deal with the blow to her life, her livelihood, her dreams.

As they pulled up in front of Willowbrook, Jed excused himself and walked away. Drew helped Beth down from the truck, his hands lingering a second longer than was necessary at her narrow waist. "I think I'm ready for that pie now. You want to join me? We can take it in the den and watch some TV."

Beth nodded. "Sure."

The kitchen was dark, the housekeeper gone for the night. But she had left the pie front and center on the table. Drew grabbed a couple of plates and cut two big slices. Beth looked askance at hers. "Seriously?"

He grinned at her, feeling the stress of the day melt away. "You're still catching up on calories. It won't hurt you. Besides, you know you're a knockout."

She blinked twice as if his words had shocked her.

Taking the can of topping, he spritzed both desserts with a fancy swirl. Since Beth was still mute, he dared to tease her. "Maybe when we know each other a little better, I'll let *you* use the whipped cream."

"In your dreams," she shot back.

But he had made her smile.

They carried their plates to the comfy den. Drew lowered the lights to a gentle glow and sat down on the sofa with a sigh of contentment. Beth took a seat beside him, but at the other end. They both kicked off their shoes and propped their feet on the coffee table.

Someone had already built a fire in the fireplace. Everyone on Drew's staff knew that as soon as the thermometer dropped below fifty for the first time in the fall, he wanted firewood and matches ASAP. It was a comfort thing to him, not so much for warmth as for the sound and smell. The pop and crackle—and the scent of burning wood. Fires reminded him of happy times with his dad...the many occasions the older Farrell had taken Jed and Drew camping in the Texas hill country.

The silence in the room was comfortable. He and Beth ate pie in harmony. It was, perhaps, a temporary détente, but he was content to enjoy the moment. Now that he was seated, the full weight of exhaustion rolled over him. Between the sleepless night and the hard, emotionally draining work in Royal today, his body felt battered.

He finished his dessert and set the plate aside. Closing his eyes, he let his head drop back against the sofa.

Beth's voice caught him just as he hovered on the edge of sleep. "How bad was it in town?"

Not bothering to move his body, he turned his head to look at her. "Bad. As bad as I've ever seen in person."

Beth was pale, her teeth worrying her bottom lip. "What did you and Jed do today?"

"Helped with the search and rescue teams. The houses we went to were all empty, but I heard that one of the crews this afternoon found a mom and two kids trapped in a bathtub with a mattress over them. They'd been yelling for help off and on for hours. But with their house crumpled on top of them, it took the dogs to sniff them out."

"But they're going to be okay?"

"Yes, thank God."

"I want to go with you tomorrow," she said.

"I understand. And there will be plenty of stuff to help with. But I'll come back for you after lunch. Jed and I have a meeting at the Cattleman's Club in the morning. Did you call the building inspector I told you about?"

Beth didn't seem entirely pleased. "I did, but I feel bad about it. Jumping to the head of the line seems rude."

"It's not rude at all. That's what friends do."

"But he's not *my* friend."

Drew sat up, rested his elbows on his knees and rubbed his eyes with his fingertips. Was he doomed to surround himself with stubborn women? He counted to ten. When he thought he had his temper under control, he glared at her. "I *know* you're an independent woman. I know you can take care of yourself. But why not let me smooth the path when I can? I guarantee that if you try to find an inspector on your own, your house will sit there for a long time. Half of Royal is going to be in the same boat."

Beth felt the pinch of shame. Drew was only trying to help. And she was being less than gracious. "I'm sorry," she said stiffly. Her mother had raised two kids on government assistance, leaving Beth with an aversion to asking for or taking help. "You're right. I'll be happy to meet with him. Thank you."

The sharp planes of Drew's masculine face softened. He reached across the cushioned no-man's-land between them and twined his fingers with hers, playing with the silver ring on her right hand. "Now, was that so hard?"

She managed a smile though she was distracted by the curve of his mouth and the way his sexy, humorous grin left her breathless. She tugged her hand away. "It must be gratifying to be able to hand out help without thinking of the consequences."

Now he frowned. "Why does that sound like an insult?"

"I wasn't being sarcastic. I'm serious. You have the means to help people without worrying about the bottom line. I imagine you find that rewarding."

He released her and returned to his earlier position. Perhaps her impulsive statement had offended him.

Shaking his head in what appeared to be disgust, he frowned. "I won't apologize for having money." The words were flat. "If you weren't so stubborn, and if you would let yourself think outside the box, you might realize that our dispute over the road could be handled in a way that would help your bottom line immensely."

This time the silence that descended was awkward. He had shut her out deliberately. Maybe she had not been entirely truthful about her lack of sarcasm. It was possible she had some passive-aggressive issues to work through when it came to the inequity between their lifestyles. But if he thought he could *buy* her automatic compliance, he was mistaken.

Drew was champagne and Rolex and jetting to Paris. Beth drank tap water, used the clock on her cheap flip phone and had never been outside of Texas. Was it any wonder that she felt at a disadvantage when it came to dealing with a macho, Texas-born-and-bred billionaire?

"May I ask you something?" she said, wanting to get inside his head and understand what made him tick.

His gaze was wary. "I suppose."

"When we were in the storm cellar, you started to tell me something about your engagement, but I cut you off. I'd really like to hear what you were going to say."

He shrugged. "It's not anything noteworthy."

"Then tell me."

He linked his hands behind his neck, staring into the fire. "Her name was Margie. We met at an equine convention in Dallas. Shared a few laughs. Tumbled into bed. We had a lot in common."

Beth pondered his response for several long seconds. "And that was enough for an engagement?"

"We went back and forth seeing each other for six months. Her condo in Houston. My place here in Royal. By the end of the seventh month, it seemed like the right time to settle down. Start a family. So I proposed. She was pleased that I asked."

"No grand passion?"

"I wouldn't call it that. No."

"Ah."

"We made it a couple of months with a ring on her finger before the problems began to crop up. She was stubborn. Extremely bull-headed."

"And so are you."

"Exactly. We locked horns about everything. If I said the sky was blue, she said it was green. Soon, every time we ended up in bed turned out to be for make-up sex."

"Some couples thrive on that."

"Not me. I started to realize that I had made a huge mistake."

"So what happened?" Beth was curious, more than she cared to admit.

Drew inhaled sharply, letting the breath out slowly. "I introduced her to a buddy of mine. Deliberately. He was from Houston. A handsome, charming veterinarian. They hit it off. Six weeks later she gave me back my ring."

"Ouch."

"But don't you see? That was what I was after. People showered me with sympathy over my "broken" engagement. I felt like a complete and utter fraud."

He turned away, perhaps already regretting his honesty. "So now you know my dirty little secret."

Several minutes passed in silence as Beth tried to analyze her confusing response to his tale. Jealousy? Relief? Sympathy? Eventually, a slight noise alerted her to a change in the status quo. Drew had fallen asleep. Poor guy.

In slumber he seemed slightly less intimidating. She studied him intently, trying to see through the handsome package to the man beneath. For months he had harassed her about selling her property to him. Even yesterday, he had approached her with fire in his eyes. But in the midst of incredible danger, he had taken control in the best possible way and made the experience of surviving a killer tornado bearable.

His dark lashes fanned out against his tanned cheeks. The broad chest that rose and fell with his regular breathing was hard and muscular. Below his belt, a taut, flat abdomen led to long legs and sock-clad feet.

Part of her was disappointed that the evening had so obviously ended. Her attraction to Drew made her want to spend time with him. But the snarky, inner Beth said *danger, danger, danger*. A girl could get her heart broken by a man like Drew Farrell.

She wondered what had happened to Jed. Drew told her he was visiting from Dallas. But the man was like a phantom. If he was in the house tonight, he was keeping to himself. Too bad. It would certainly help to have a third party around. Someone who might be able to keep Beth and Drew from either strangling each other or tumbling into bed without weighing the consequences.

A gentle snore from the man on the couch made her smile in spite of her unsettled emotions. Drew was out for the count. He would probably sleep better in his own bed, but Beth definitely didn't feel comfortable poking his leg and suggesting that he move. In lieu of that, she stood quietly, removed the fire screen, and added a couple more logs to the blaze.

Warming her hands, she studied the dancing flames. Already, she felt the pull of Willowbrook Farms. It was a warm, welcoming place, something she had never experienced growing up. She'd never slept on the street, but a home was more than brick and mortar. A home meant security and comfort. Beth and her brother had battled uncertainty and fear more times than not.

Shaking off the bad memories, she turned for one last wistful look at her would-be benefactor. She couldn't afford to depend on Drew. She'd already had one man give her a helping hand. But at least back then, she'd been a broke college student, so there was some basis for taking what had been a huge gift.

Now, she was an adult woman who paid her bills on time and took care of herself. If she weakened and let Drew do too much, her self-respect would become an issue. Not only that, but there was a good chance he was trying to soften her up. Maybe he thought if she were beholden to him it would be easier to sway her to his way of thinking. Because she was attracted to him, the situation was even more fraught with pitfalls. If and when the two of them ever pursued what she now knew was a definite spark, she wanted a level playing field. A relationship of equals.

Unfortunately, that was never going to happen. No matter how you spun the fantasy, she didn't belong in Drew's world. She was the girl from the wrong side of the tracks.

Six

Drew struggled to stay focused on the conversation ping-ponging around the large conference table. Every man and woman in the room was a friend of his. And they were all well-respected members of the Texas Cattleman's Club. At Sheriff Nathan Battle's request, the informal group had convened to discuss the coordination of cleanup efforts and the utilization of volunteers now that the county had been designated a disaster area.

Nathan looked as if he hadn't slept at all. Drew himself had awakened at 3:00 a.m. to a cold, empty living room. The fire had long since burned out, and Beth was nowhere to be found. He'd dragged himself to his bed and managed a few more hours, but he'd been up at first light, eager to get into town and assess the situation.

The trouble was, though he was here, all he could think about was Beth. He'd left the keys to the truck he had promised her with the housekeeper. And Allan was supposed to be at Beth's place at 10:00. But even so, Drew felt a churning in his gut that told him he was more invested in Beth's situation than was wise.

Forcing himself to concentrate, he was startled when his buddy Whit Daltry whispered in his right ear.

"I helped rescue Megan's daughter, Evie, from the day-care center yesterday. It was chaos. All those terrified parents and kids. I can't imagine what Megan was going through."

Drew muttered softly in return. "I thought you and Megan were mortal enemies."

"Very funny." Whit rubbed two fingers in the center of the forehead as if he had a headache. And he probably did. "Things change, Drew. Especially now."

The talk at the table had moved to an even more sober topic. Funerals. There would be a number of them over the next week. Fortunately, the mortuary and Royal's three main churches had sustained only minimal damage.

Drew spoke up at one point. "Jed and I would like to donate $100,000 to start a fund for families with no insurance." One by one, people jumped in, offering similar amounts as they were able. A representative from social services suggested designating a point person to triage which needs were most urgent.

Shelter would be the first priority. And then cleanup.

The enormity of the task was mind-boggling. Drew looked around the table at Royal residents he had known since childhood, people who pulled together in times of trouble. The town had never faced a catastrophe of this magnitude. But together they would rebuild and help the helpless.

The building in which they sat, the Texas Cattleman's Club, was an icon in Royal. Built in the early 1900s, it had served as a gathering place for movers and shakers, primarily ranchers whose families had owned their property for decades. Though once upon a time a bastion for the *good ole boys,* the club in recent years had moved into the twenty-first century.

Despite opposition from the old guard, the club had begun admitting female members. Not only that, the TCC had opened an onsite day care center. Times were changing. The old ways were beginning to coexist with the new. Both had something to offer.

As a historical and social landmark, the TCC was an integral part of the town's identity. Fortunately, the main building had survived the tornado, but downed trees had damaged many of the outbuildings. Broken glass and water damage seemed to be the worst of the problems.

Gil Addison was on his feet now. "I think I speak for everyone in this room, Nathan, when I say that we'll do whatever it takes, for however long it takes. As each of you leaves in a few moments, my assistant will be at a table outside taking volunteer sign-ups for shifts on various work details. I know most of us will have some personal issues to deal with, but I appreciate whatever you can do for the town. Because we *are* the town."

Applause broke out as the meeting ended.

Jed ran a hand through his hair and turned to Drew. "I brought work clothes with me. What if you and I grab a bite of lunch and then I'll stay here while you go get Beth?"

"Sounds like a plan. Do you think Kimberly will want to help, too?"

A funny look crossed Jed's face. "I don't think she's free this afternoon."

Drew felt as if there was something going on there, but he had too much to juggle on his own without sticking his nose into Jed's life. He was just glad his brother had been in Royal and not Dallas when the tornado hit. It felt good to have Jed's support at a time like this.

On the way out, Drew paused to speak to friends: Stella Daniels from the mayor's office, who was playing a key role dealing with the media, and Keaton Holt, who co-owned and ran the Holt Cattle Ranch. Everyone's demeanor was the same. Grief, determination, and beneath it all, a pervasive sense of loss. The tragedy had stripped away a semblance of security and left them all floundering.

Drew signed up for a shift later in the day and spoke briefly with Nathan, reporting the damage to Beth's home. When he finally made it to his truck, he waited for Jed to grab his things. "I think I'll take a pass on lunch," he said. "I want to catch Allen, the inspector, if he's still around and hear the report on Beth's house."

Jed nodded. "I'll give you a rain check. Say hi to Beth for me…and don't do anything I wouldn't do."

Beth felt a trickle of sweat roll down her back. There wasn't a cloud in the sky, with temperatures reaching the lower eighties. That was Texas for you. A veritable smorgasbord of weather. For the first hour, she had been banned from the house while the inspector, hardhat in place, went over the structure with a fine-tooth comb.

At last, he permitted her to enter. He took her around, pointing out spots that would require repair. Fortunately, the foundation was intact. That was a huge relief.

Beth put her hands on her hips and frowned. "So if I had to sleep here, I could?"

Drew's buddy frowned. "Well, in theory, yes. But it should be a last resort. You'd be breathing in bits of insulation and maybe mold in the short term. I wouldn't recommend it." He clicked a few more times on his hand-held tablet and pursed his lips. "I should be able to get you this report by tomorrow morning. If you call your insurance immediately and give them my contact info, we can get the ball rolling. Hopefully, you'll be near the front of the line."

"Thank you for coming."

He climbed in his car and lowered the window to say goodbye. "It won't be so bad. To a layperson, this might look daunting, but a professional carpenter will have you back to rights in no time. I'll be in touch."

As the inspector drove back down the driveway toward the shared road that had been a bone of contention between Beth and Drew, she wondered for a bleak half second if she should simply sell her land to Drew and relocate. She'd poured what little capital she had into making a go of Green Acres. It would take months to recover from this setback. Maybe it would be smarter to look for a small house in town.

She had worked at the bank before. It wasn't her passion, but it paid the bills.

As she stood there pondering her options, a second vehicle arrived, this one an ancient green Pinto with a muffler that was shot. The car shuddered and snorted to a stop. Beth's stomach clenched. The last thing she needed today was a run-in with her deadbeat brother.

The car door opened and Audie stepped out. He weighed barely a hundred pounds sopping wet. Numerous jail sentences over the last ten years had hardened him. Mostly B&E, with a few disorderly conducts and a handful of public drunkenness thrown in. Audie had his mother's alcoholic tendencies. Unfortunately, she'd let him drink his first beer at age twelve. It was a wonder he wasn't already dead from liver failure.

Audie had been in and out of rehab repeatedly. But apparently this last time had produced some success. Though Beth found it difficult to trust anything he said, Audie had supposedly been clean for six months now.

Beth had done her best to rise above the stigma of her upbringing. Hanging out with her brother didn't help matters. But as much as she hated his behavior and his lack of backbone, she couldn't ignore the fact that he had a wife and child.

Angie, Audie's bride of four years, was a cheerful woman-child with less street smarts than most kindergarteners. What she saw in Audie was anyone's guess. The baby was small and sad-eyed, but as far as Beth could tell, little Anton was healthy. Angie had picked out the decidedly non-Texan name. She liked having three *A*s in the family.

Angie and Anton remained in the car, so that meant this visit was business and not pleasure. Beth's stomach knotted. She had called her brother to check on him only this morning and gotten his answering machine.

When she made no effort to approach the parked car, Audie ambled in her direction. "Hey, sis." When he smiled, the usual sly calculation in his gaze was missing. He appeared clear-eyed and sober. "Looks like the house is okay."

She raised her eyebrows, incredulous. "An entire section is gone."

He shrugged. "Still standing. Our apartment is toast. Thought we might stay with you for a while."

"Audie...." She struggled for words. Bringing in a homeless stranger would be an easier task than dealing with her sibling's personality.

"C'mon," he said, slinging an arm around her shoulder. "We're family. You wouldn't let a baby sleep on the streets, would you?"

Feeling boxed in and frustrated, Beth evaded his grasp. "There are shelters set up in town."

"Those are for people who don't have relatives to help out. I got you, babe." His snickered reference to an old song didn't amuse Beth in the least.

"I'll have to get repairs done. Construction debris is no place for a child."

"We can stay out in the shed. It has electricity and a sink. And a utility shower."

It was clear that Audie had made up his mind. Beth knew from experience he would continue to harangue her until she gave in. Perhaps she shouldn't stay in Royal at all. Sometimes the temptation to move far away and make a new start was compelling. This setback in her fledgling farm endeavor might be a sign.

But in the same instant, she thought of Drew. And of her friends and neighbors in Royal who faced a long road ahead. This corner of Texas was all Beth had ever known. Though her memories of growing up weren't entirely positive, Royal was home. Audie would always be her brother, no matter how hard she tried to tell herself they were nothing alike. They shared DNA and a difficult past.

Audie had made different choices in life than Beth had. Poor choices in many instances. She felt no real compunction about letting him bear the consequences of his actions. But she couldn't turn her back on an innocent child and a waiflike woman with no common sense at all.

"Fine," she said. "Have it your way. You can stay. But you'll have to bring in some kind of camp stove and a mini fridge."

"Why didn't you take care of that?" he asked.

"I'm not staying here," she said evenly. "Drew Farrell has invited me to Willowbrook Farms for as long as it takes me to get the repairs done."

Audie frowned. Apparently he had assumed Beth would be responsible for everything. "Well, that's convenient. Seems like you always have men hanging around to look after you."

The implication in his voice and in his words made her furious, but she wouldn't let him see that he could get to her. Keeping her expression bland, she lifted an eyebrow. "Audie…"

"Yeah?"

"For once in your life, try to think of someone other than yourself. If this turns out to be too uncomfortable for Angie and Anton, please be a man and find a solution."

"Easy for you to say."

She refused to let him make her feel guilty. "I'm leaving now." She headed toward the green Pinto to greet her nephew and sister-in-law. But before she got there, a familiar dark truck turned off the highway and approached the house. *Well, this day just keeps getting better and better.* Grim-faced, she watched Drew Farrell park and get out of his vehicle.

He lifted a hand as he approached. "Has Allen already come and gone?"

She nodded. "I'm surprised you didn't pass him. It hasn't been that long."

Drew stopped short, seeing Audie and the car. He held out a hand. "I'm Drew Farrell. Don't believe I know you."

Audie wiped his palm on his jeans before returning the gesture and shaking Drew's hand. "I'm Audie Andrews, Beth's brother."

Beth knew Drew well enough by now to see that he was surprised. But he hid it well. "I suppose you're checking up on your sister."

Audie seemed nonplussed, possibly because the notion of worrying about anyone other than himself was foreign to him. "Um…yeah."

"Did she tell you what happened?"

"You mean the tornado?"

Drew smothered a smile, exchanging a quick look with Beth. "Not just that. Obviously the farm took a direct hit. But we were trapped in the storm cellar overnight. The car pinned us inside." The vehicle in question still sat in a forlorn heap. Beth wondered if it was worth anything as scrap metal.

Audie's eyes shifted from Drew to Beth. "You two must be kinda close."

"We're neighbors." Drew's wry smile dared Beth to disagree. "I had come over to discuss a few things with Beth when the sirens went off."

"And now she's staying at your house."

It was hard to miss the insinuation. Beth's cheeks burned with humiliation. There were about a thousand places she would rather be right now than in the midst of this awkward confrontation.

Drew ignored the provocative statement and returned his attention to Beth. "What did Allen have to say?"

"He hopes to have his report to me by tomorrow morning. The foundation is sound. He says the other stuff won't be as bad as it looks to repair."

"That's great."

"It is."

Surely Drew was confused about her lack of enthusiasm, but she was barely holding it together. Her nerves were shot. Dealing with Audie always had that effect on her. She grimaced as she faced her brother. "I have to go now. Make yourself at home."

Drew gaped. "They're staying here?"

Audie cocked his head toward the car. "I'm between jobs at the moment. Our place in town was trashed by the storm. But we were only rentin' anyway, and it's the end of the month. Beth is going to let us bunk down out in the shed. It's in pretty good shape. We'll be fine."

Beth noticed he didn't bother to mention that he'd been fired from his last two places of employment for showing up drunk.

Drew seemed baffled. This unfortunate intersection of the haves and the have-nots illustrated more than anything else the gulf between Beth's world and the Farrell empire.

She interceded, hoping to end the regrettable interlude. "I have to go, Audie. Drew and I are volunteering in town this afternoon."

Excusing herself, she went to say hello to Angie and Anton and then returned quickly to Drew's side. "Shall I follow you?" she asked.

Drew's gaze went from Beth to Audie and back again. "We can change our plan," he said, his expression troubled.

"It's not necessary. I want to go into town and do something useful."

A long silence stretched to thirty seconds. Maybe more. For once, Audie kept his mouth shut. Finally, Drew's shoulders lifted and fell. "Okay, then. We'll stop by the ranch to grab a bite to eat and drop off the clunker. Then we'll go."

Perhaps it escaped Drew's notice that his version of a *clunker* was several notches above Audie's car.

Beth wiped sweat from her forehead with the back of her hand, wishing she had thought to bring water. "Goodbye, Audie."

He nodded. "Thanks for letting us stay."

Beth took Drew's arm. "Let's go."

When they were out of earshot, he opened her door and muttered beneath his breath. "Are you sure we don't need to do something for them? They're your family."

She closed her eyes briefly and took a deep breath, settling her hands on the steering wheel. "Audie always lands on his feet. He's the perfect example of *give him an inch and he'll take a mile*. Don't worry about them. They'll be fine. I swear."

Turning the key in the ignition, she made her wishes clear. "It's getting late."

To her dismay, Drew stood at her window for several long seconds. He must think she was a heartless bitch. But for the life of her, she didn't have the energy to explain why Audie was a barnacle on the ship that was her life.

The truth was, he was *worse* than a barnacle. Barnacles didn't actually do any damage. But Audie wreaked havoc in his wake. Even sober, he was an opportunist and a liar.

Without another word, she raised her window, turned on the air conditioning and spun gravel as she shot down the drive and onto the road. Her eyes burned with tears. She swallowed hard, blinking them away. She refused to let Drew see how much her brother upset her.

Drew couldn't possibly understand what it was like to crawl out of a dismal past and reach for something cleaner, something better. Was that a crime?

The thought of Audie staying at Green Acres outraged her, despite the fact that the house was ripped apart and vulnerable. She knew there was a good chance that before she managed to eventually evict him, he would steal anything worth pawning. It had happened before...far too often.

Angie would never know. She was so clueless, it never occurred to her to ask where Audie got the money he spent so recklessly. And Beth wouldn't say a word. Because she had *been* Anton once upon a time. A helpless child at the mercy of a parent too selfish and irresponsible to make sure she was safe.

The only way to cope at the moment was to compartmentalize. This afternoon, she and Drew were going to offer assistance where they could. In the midst of tragedy they would extend a helping hand. If Drew wanted to talk about Audie, Beth would deflect the conversation.

Seven

Drew followed Beth back to Willowbrook, wondering what in the hell was going on. Beth had never mentioned Audie, but now that Drew thought about it, she *had* alluded to her family not being close. Maybe her brother was the only family she had. Clearly, the two of them didn't get along.

Was she embarrassed for Drew to meet Audie? Maybe she thought Drew was the kind of man to pass judgment on others. He knew full well that he was a very fortunate guy. He'd been born into a loving family, one with considerable financial assets. Though his parents had retired early and moved to Padre Island, all of the Farrells were a close-knit group, even the cousins and aunts and uncles.

As he parked and got out of his truck, Beth was already hurrying up the front steps. By the time he reached the kitchen, he found her talking to the housekeeper, who was quickly setting out lunch.

Suddenly starved, Drew sat down and dug into a thick corned beef sandwich. The afternoon would be more about physical labor than the morning had been. Breakfast was a long time ago. Beth seemed equally hungry, but she barely glanced at him as she ate.

She finished before he did and gave him a smile that didn't reach her eyes. Blotting her mouth with a napkin, she stood. "If you'll excuse me, I want to freshen up for a moment before I leave. I'll see you back here tonight."

He caught her wrist. "It doesn't make sense for both of us to drive. I'll take you anywhere you want to go."

Not a muscle in her body moved. She stared away from him. Beneath his thumb, her pulse was rapid. "Fine. If you're sure."

Releasing her reluctantly, he nodded. "I'll be ready in fifteen minutes."

She disappeared, leaving him to ponder the odds that she would actually wait for him. Maybe she was upset about dealing with her brother. Families could be complicated. Most likely, Audie's unemployment made things worse.

When Drew stepped out onto the front porch two minutes ahead of his deadline, Beth was perched on the top step. Despite the heat, she was wearing faded jeans that would protect her legs. A yellow cotton sunhat perched on top of her head. Her long, blond curls were tucked up in a jaunty ponytail. She smelled of sunscreen.

He touched her shoulder briefly. "Let's go. Where would you like me to drop you?"

Beth shot him a sideways glance as they climbed into the overly-warm cab of the truck. "I'd like to check on Megan at the animal shelter."

Drew cranked up the A/C, wondering if Mother Nature realized that it was October. The temperature was supposed to be winding down. "Are the two of you friends?"

"Recent friends." Beth's gaze was pensive as she stared through the windshield. "When I first moved to the farm, it felt lonely at night. Megan helped me adopt a sweet puppy. His name was Gus. Half cocker spaniel, the other half pure mischief. I built a fenced-in enclosure, but he got out one day. One of my customers ran over him."

Without thinking about it, Drew reached across the small space that separated them and touched her hand. "That sucks. I'm really sorry."

She didn't look at him, and she moved her hand. "I felt so guilty."

"You shouldn't. That's what puppies do. They get loose. And run out into the road. Sometimes it doesn't end well. Did you ever think about getting a second dog?"

"For about two seconds. Love can't be transferred automatically, you know. I loved Gus. But maybe I don't need a pet. I'm having a hard enough time taking care of myself."

She said it matter-of-factly, and now Drew was the one who felt guilty. Here was a woman who had battled long odds to pursue a dream. But he'd overlooked her hard work and dismissed her modest success in his single-minded determination to safeguard his horses and his business.

From Beth's perspective, he must have seemed like an arrogant jerk. He chewed on that unpalatable bone until they pulled up in front of Royal Safe Haven. The animal shelter was located near the hospital in an industrial area of town.

Beth scanned the premises. "It looks like they've been spared."

"It's hard to believe, because the hospital lost an entire wing. But it was the oldest section, so maybe it wasn't up to modern codes."

The grounds of the shelter were covered in tree limbs and foliage and debris carried in from parts unknown. But the single story brick structure appeared solid.

Megan McGuiness, the owner, greeted them with a harried expression. "Thank God. I hope at least one of you is here to lend a hand. People have been dropping off strays all morning." The green-eyed, curvy woman was pale beneath her sprinkling of freckles. Her straight, bright red hair framed her face in tangles.

Beth hugged her, despite the assortment of stains on the other woman's clothing. "Drew is committed to a work detail in town. But I can stay for a while."

"Bless you." Megan arched her back and winced. "The animals went nuts. Clearly there was no way to get them all in a storm shelter. I'm grateful we escaped the worst of it."

Beth turned to Drew. "I still want to see the damage in the rest of Royal. And help if I can. But I'd like to stay here with Megan for a couple of hours. Would you mind coming back to get me?"

"Of course not." He focused his attention on Megan. "Is there anything you need in terms of supplies? Anything I could round up in town?"

"Some tarps would be great, but I have a feeling those are going to be scarce as hen's teeth. Still, I'll take what you can get. And a roll of twine."

He grinned. "Beth can text me if you think of anything else."

Megan's smile turned sly. "What I really need is adoptive homes. How would you feel about taking a couple of cats, Drew?"

He grimaced. "I'm allergic to cats."

"They're barn cats. You have a barn. It's a match made in heaven."

Beth held up her hands when Drew blanched. "Don't look at me," she said. "My house is barely standing. It's no place for an animal right now."

Drew gave in with good grace. He and Megan had gone out once about a hundred years ago, so he cared about her...though more as a sister. "Fine. Two cats. No more. I'll send one of my guys to pick them up this afternoon if I can find anyone who's not working cleanup."

Megan went up on tiptoe to kiss his cheek. "I knew there was a reason I liked you."

He rolled his eyes. "Flattery doesn't work on me. I've already agreed to the deal. You don't have to oversell it."

Beth chuckled. "You'd better run, Drew. The last time I was here she had two iguanas and a python. I think you're getting off easy."

Beth smiled at her friend as Drew drove away. "I should have already asked. How is Evie?" Beth had met the four-year-old when Beth had adopted the puppy. Evie's precocious charm had won her over immediately.

Some emotion flickered in Megan's eyes. "She's good. She's fine."

Since the other woman's tone of voice indicated she didn't want to talk further about her child, Beth backed off. "Tell me what to do. I know you're overwhelmed."

For the first time, Megan took a deep breath, her gaze sober. "Is it true that your house is badly damaged?"

Beth nodded. "My place took a direct hit. The fields are ruined. One corner of the house is a shambles. Drew and I were trapped in the storm cellar overnight when my car decided to land on top of us."

"Dear Lord."

"Yes. We were lucky. I still get shaky thinking about it."

"Well, I can take your mind off your troubles, I guarantee. Come on inside and you can help me decide how to rig up some extra cages. I won't be able to use the outdoor dog runs until I get help clearing everything the storm dropped on top of us."

Within the walls of the building, chaos reigned. Dogs howled. Cats screeched. It was as if the animals realized that a disaster of epic proportions had swept the county. And perhaps they did.

When Beth voiced the thought, Megan nodded. "They understand, they really do. Dogs and cats are remarkably intuitive. Of course, right now most of them are cranky because their routines have been altered. But they'll settle down soon. I hope."

For the next couple of hours, Beth worked until her back was sore and her legs ached. Feeding and watering the clientele took a long time, not to mention finding places for the new residents displaced by the storm.

At one point, pausing to catch her breath, she leaned down and picked up a tiny puppy with matted golden-brown hair. He reminded her a lot of Gus. The little dog curled into her arms with what she could swear was a sigh of relief. Murmuring to her newfound friend, she stroked his ears. "If you don't have a name, I'll call you Stormy. I know…it's cliché. But all the little girl dogs will think you're cute."

Megan returned from outside where she had been hosing out buckets. "Looks like somebody loves you."

Beth's heart turned over in a wistful flip of longing. "Do me a favor, Megan."

"Of course."

"If no one comes to claim this sweet fella, will you keep him for me? Until I'm back in my house?"

"I doubt Drew would care if you brought a dog home. He's not allergic to those. The man has a Golden Retriever and a couple of Bluetick hounds."

"All the more reason to leave Stormy here. Drew is already feeding and housing me. I can't trespass on his good nature any further than that."

Megan lifted an eyebrow. "You're *staying* with Drew? I thought he was the big bad wolf trying to gobble up your farm."

Beth held Stormy more tightly. "It's not like that. When

he saw that my house was going to need major repairs, he offered me a room. That's all."

Megan grinned. "And how many other homeless females has he taken in?"

"None."

"I rest my case."

At that exact moment, a horn honked outside, signaling Drew's return. He carried in the supplies Megan had requested and glanced at Beth with amusement. "You both look like you've been dragged through a bush backward."

"*Some* of us have been working hard," she said.

He didn't rise to the bait. "You ready to go?" He scratched Stormy's tummy gently. The puppy practically rolled his eyes in ecstasy. Beth understood entirely. Drew's big hands gave a woman naughty ideas.

Beth looked at Megan and handed over the small dog. "I'll come back again, I promise."

Megan tucked the pup under her arm and glanced at her utilitarian watch. "No worries. We've had lots of volunteers. Thanks for all you've done."

Drew pointed the truck toward downtown. "You sure you want to do this?" The farther they drove, the more damage they witnessed. Beth stared in silence. At one point he saw a single tear slide down her cheek. But she didn't wipe it away.

"How can it happen so fast?" she asked, the words heartbroken.

He understood that it was a rhetorical question. Though he had already seen the devastation yesterday and twice today, the senseless destruction still took his breath away. The random patterns of the storm's fury played out much like what they had seen at Beth's farm. Some streets were still impassable, cordoned off by orange and white barricades. Power poles had been tumbled like matchsticks.

But in the midst of chaos, here and there, a potted plant survived…a child's bicycle, a glass shop front. Signs of hope in the midst of incredible sorrow. Drew pointed to a family of four sifting through what was left of their modest two-story home. "Everywhere I've gone so far, people have been amazing. They're putting it in perspective. Grateful to have each other." Left unspoken was the thought that not everyone had survived.

"Where are we going?" Beth asked, her voice subdued.

"The high school. They've set up a large shelter area in the gym. How do you feel about reading books to kids?"

"I have no idea. I'm never really around little ones very much."

"I'm in the same boat, but this came as a direct request from the shelter coordinator. They've provided phone service and internet connections so parents can deal with insurance details and anything else. But it's hard for the children to be cooped up. Schools are going to be closed for at least a week, probably longer. The principal is lining up volunteers to plan activities and give some structure to the days."

"I'll do whatever I can."

When they entered the gym, normally open to the community for basketball games and carnival nights, the scene was a cacophony of loud voices and crying children. Cots lined the floor in neat rows. It struck Drew that if he hadn't asked Beth to stay with him, she might have been a resident here as well. He couldn't imagine trying to keep a family together and entertained in the midst of such chaos.

Thankfully, it appeared that social services and law enforcement were handling this very personal disaster efficiently and compassionately. Emergency preparedness training had kicked in, and relief efforts were functioning like a well-oiled machine.

Drew steered Beth toward a far corner that served as command central. The site coordinator's face lit up when she saw them. "You're a gift from heaven," she said. "The TCC members have been amazing. We've already started three age groups with other volunteers. I'd like the two of you to take the eight, nine and ten-year-olds to classroom 107. There are fifteen of them in all. You'll find signs in the hallway directing you. Someone will deliver afternoon snacks." She handed Beth a copy of *Charlotte's Web* and two other books. "Thank you."

That was the extent of their training. Drew smiled at Beth ruefully. "Ready for this?"

She was rumpled and hot and her ponytail was awry. But her beautiful eyes sparked with mischief. "I can handle anything you dish out. Bring it on."

In moments, they were surrounded by a gaggle of youngsters chattering excitedly—except for the few whose sober faces reflected a very adult understanding of all they had lost. One little boy with a crooked haircut and pants that were too short held Drew's hand as they walked down the hall.

Beth took the lead, playing the role of Pied Piper as they led their charges to the assigned spot. It didn't take long to get the kids settled into their desks. The furniture was designed for adolescents, which was a novelty in itself. When a momentary quiet reigned, Beth lifted an eyebrow, holding up one of the books.

Drew shook his head. "I'll be bad cop, if necessary. You take the wheel."

Shaking her head with a wry smile, she took the teacher's chair, pulled it from behind the large oak desk and sat down facing her audience. If she was nervous, she didn't show it. After reading quietly through the first few paragraphs, she found her rhythm and injected a note of drama into Fern's character, particularly the girl's outrage when she found out the small pig was going to be killed.

At that moment, Drew realized his role as disciplinarian was going to be unnecessary. The children hung on Beth's every word. She read nonstop for forty-five minutes, creating voices for each new actor in the beloved story. Even Drew found himself caught up in the classic tale.

But after a while he went from listening to watching. The curve of Beth's lips as she smiled. The nuances of expression on her face. The way she made eye contact with each child, as if assuring every boy and girl that she was reading just to him or her.

It struck him that Beth Andrews would make an amazing mother. Drew hadn't spent much time thinking about marriage and babies and home and hearth. After all, he was only thirty-two. He had plenty of time.

But the storm's havoc made him reassess a lot of things. Watching families pull together in the last forty-eight hours had shown him the importance of being grounded. Jed lived in Dallas, their parents in south Texas. Drew travelled often. Though his work was satisfying and he had a wide circle of friends and extended relatives, for the first time he wondered if he was missing something very important. Maybe he needed to think about the bigger picture.

Beth ended a chapter as the promised refreshments arrived. Supervising snack time was a sticky, rowdy mess, but it reminded him of what it was like to be a kid. When the apples and peanut butter disappeared faster than a snowflake in the hot sun, he helped clean up the debris. Another volunteer arrived to shepherd the group of children back to their parents.

Drew straightened one last row of seats and grinned at

Beth. "Your talents are lost on farming. You should have been either a librarian or an actress."

Tucking wayward strands of hair behind her ears, she perched on the teacher's desk, her legs swinging. "To be honest, kids give me the heebie-jeebies. They scare me to death. One wrong word or move, and you've scarred them for life. It's too much responsibility. And as for being an actress, well…let's just say I prefer digging in the dirt."

He yawned and stretched, feeling tired but content. "It's hard to believe that forty-eight hours ago we were running for our lives."

"I know. It seems like a dream until you look outside. Then it smacks you in the face. I feel so sorry for all the people taking shelter here. Especially the ones with children. My house is damaged, but at least I have only myself to worry about."

"And your brother."

Beth's face closed up. "I don't want to talk about Audie."

"We're one man short at the stables. I could offer him a job. It's grunt work…doesn't pay much. But it would be better than nothing."

Despite the stuffy air in the classroom, Beth's pink cheeks paled. "That would be a very bad idea. Trust me." Her soft lips firmed in a grim line.

"It's not that big a deal. I really am looking for somebody."

"Then look somewhere else."

He stood, nonplussed, and wondered with a sick feeling in the pit of his stomach if Beth was as stubborn and intractable as his ex-fiancée. Whatever happened to sweet, amenable women?

Beth jumped down from the desk and walked toward the door. "We should see if they need us anywhere else."

"Wait." The command came out more urgently than he had intended.

Beth stopped and turned. Her posture was wary. "What's wrong?"

He went to her and rubbed a thumb over her cheek. "I've been wondering if those first two kisses were a fluke."

When her gaze went to his mouth, a tingle of something hot and heady settled in his gut.

She bit her lip. "Perhaps not flukes, but probably mistakes. Adrenaline…the will to live. That's all."

"Don't kid yourself, Beth. I haven't been able to stop thinking about them." He slid one hand beneath her hair, prepared to draw back if she made a protest. Instead, she looked up at him with curiosity and something more. It was that second emotion that stole his breath and made his hands shake.

Lowering his head, he found her lips with his. She tasted like peanut butter and cherry Kool-Aid. At first, her arms hung at her sides. He explored her mouth gently, his tongue brushing hers. The only other place their bodies connected was where his left hand cupped her chin.

In the storm cellar, emotions had run high. Now, in the broad light of day, he felt the same jolt of arousal. "Touch me," he said.

Slowly, her arms came up and twined around his neck. She stretched on her tiptoes, straining to get closer.

Lifting her off her feet, he strode to the teacher's desk and sat her there, moving into the V of her thighs. Now they were perfectly matched. He cupped her breast through her shirt. The door was unlocked. They were in a public building. Though he rubbed his thumb over her nipple, he knew he dared not go any further.

"I don't know what to do with you," he muttered.

She rested her forehead on his collarbone. "I have a few ideas."

Her droll humor startled a laugh from him. "I hope we're on the same page."

Her answer was to kiss him so sweetly that an entirely inopportune erection was the result. Breathing heavily, he stepped away, trying to elude temptation. "I think one of us is supposed to say this is going too fast."

She shrugged, leaning back on her hands. "I've had a terrible crush on you for over a year, even when you *were* being an obnoxious, overbearing plutocrat."

"Ouch." His wince was not feigned. Hearing her description of his less-than-stellar qualities made him squirm. "I thought we called a truce."

"Under duress and the threat of apocalypse."

"Then I'll say it again," he muttered quietly. "For the moment, I'm not going to fight with you or try to make you see reason."

She crooked a finger. He went to her like a kite on a string, hoping she didn't recognize the hold she had on him.

Beth kissed him again, but in a naughtier fashion this time. She pulled back and smiled, her lips swollen. "We're consenting adults. I'm staying at your house temporarily. Seems like the universe is giving us a sign."

He curled a hand behind her neck and pulled her mouth to his, no longer as in control as he would have liked. "If you believe in that kind of stuff."

"Are you turning me down?"

He jerked. "Hell, no. Besides, this was *my* idea."

"To-*may*-to, to-*mah*-to. But if we're going to share the credit, then we'll both share the blame when we crash and burn."

"Why would you say a thing like that?" He stole half

a second to nip her earlobe with sharp teeth. Her groaned sigh was his reward.

"You're you, and I'm me," she whispered with inescapable logic.

"So?"

"Don't ruin the moment, Farrell. We're the definition of short-term."

He sighed. "I don't want to argue about what ifs. Surely the tornado taught us that. Live in the moment. Carpe diem. Any cliché you want to choose. I've never come that close to disaster. I feel foolish saying it, but it changed me."

Beth stared at him, her green eyes bright. He wondered what she was thinking.

Finally she responded. "I think it's too soon to make a statement like that. Give it a week. A month. You'll be your old self."

"That's pretty cynical."

"People don't change, Drew."

"Are we talking about your brother again?"

"Let me get one thing straight. If you and I are contemplating a hook-up, there have to be ground rules. Number one is *forget about my brother.*"

"That's pretty cold."

"Take it or leave it. I don't tell you how to run your ranch. Please respect my wishes."

"And if it turns out to be more than a hook-up?"

"It won't. I won't let it. I like you, Drew. A lot. When you're not trying to push me around, you're funny and sexy and way too handsome for your own good. But long-term relationships are built on shared backgrounds and values."

"You think we don't have the same values?"

She stood up and straightened her clothing. "I think we're done here." She walked past him to the door and turned. "Are you coming with me?"

He grimaced. "I'll be a few minutes behind you."

She looked confused until she noticed the front of his pants. Her face flushed. "Ah. Well then. Okay."

Despite his physical discomfort, he had to chuckle when she left the room. Beth Andrews tried so hard to pretend she was a badass, but he knew the truth now. Her tough exterior concealed a woman who had perhaps been hurt one too many times. What she didn't know, however, was that Drew Farrell was a patient man. Sooner or later he would prove to her that the two of them were much more alike than she thought.

And when they ended up in bed during the process, he was pretty sure there were going to be fireworks and bells and enough heat to rival the Texas sun.

YOUR PARTICIPATION IS REQUESTED!

Dear Reader,

Since you are a lover of our books – we would like to get to know you!

Inside you will find a short Reader's Survey. Sharing your answers with us will help our editorial staff understand who you are and what activities you enjoy.

To thank you for your participation, we would like to send you 2 books and 2 gifts – **ABSOLUTELY FREE!**

Enjoy your gifts with our appreciation,

Pam Powers

**SEE INSIDE
FOR READER'S
SURVEY**

For Your Reading Pleasure...

YOUR READER'S SURVEY
"THANK YOU" FREE GIFTS INCLUDE:
- ▶ 2 FREE books
- ▶ 2 lovely surprise gifts

PLEASE FILL IN THE CIRCLES COMPLETELY TO RESPOND

1) What type of fiction books do you enjoy reading? (Check all that apply)
- ○ Suspense/Thrillers
- ○ Action/Adventure
- ○ Modern-day Romances
- ○ Historical Romance
- ○ Humour
- ○ Paranormal Romance

2) What attracted you most to the last fiction book you purchased on impulse?
- ○ The Title
- ○ The Cover
- ○ The Author
- ○ The Story

3) What is usually the greatest influencer when you <u>plan</u> to buy a book?
- ○ Advertising
- ○ Referral
- ○ Book Review

4) How often do you access the internet?
- ○ Daily
- ○ Weekly
- ○ Monthly
- ○ Rarely or never

5) How many NEW paperback fiction novels have you purchased in the past 3 months?
- ○ 0 - 2
- ○ 3 - 6
- ○ 7 or more

YES! I have completed the Reader's Survey. Please send me the 2 FREE books and 2 FREE gifts (gifts are worth about $10) for which I qualify. I understand that I am under no obligation to purchase any books, as explained on the back of this card.

225/326 HDL GGCS

FIRST NAME

LAST NAME

ADDRESS

APT.#

CITY

STATE/PROV.

ZIP/POSTAL CODE

EMAIL

© 2014 HARLEQUIN ENTERPRISES LIMITED
® and ™ are trademarks owned and used by the trademark owner and/or its licensee. Printed in the U.S.A.

HD-914-SUR-13

▲ If offer card is missing write to: Harlequin Reader Service, P.O. Box 1867, Buffalo, NY 14240-1867 or visit www.ReaderService.com ▲

Eight

Beth navigated the gym, stopping to talk to a few people she recognized. Despite the circumstances, the large room felt comfortable and safe. Because so many families were in the same boat, a sense of camaraderie permeated the air.

Nobody was perfect. Tempers flared occasionally, and children fussed when they were tired and hungry. Without asking, Beth joined the line of volunteers helping serve a simple spaghetti dinner. Folding tables—hastily set up—accommodated the large crowd in shifts. She watched the hallway that led to the school proper and knew the moment Drew reappeared.

His eyes scanned the room. She couldn't tell if he saw her or not. Instead of crossing the gym in her direction, he spoke with the site coordinator and was soon climbing a very tall ladder to replace lightbulbs on the ceiling.

Beth loved the way he walked and moved. He was confident, masculine and strong. Drew was the kind of man who should have at least a couple of kids, maybe more. He would be an incredible father. Beth had no memory of her father, so she didn't have much personal basis for comparison. But she knew that things like compassion and generosity and gentleness were important.

While she had read *Charlotte's Web* to the group of children, one small boy had climbed without fanfare into

Drew's lap. Far from seeming uncomfortable, Drew had murmured something to the kid and curled an arm around his waist.

Witnessing that moment had twisted something in Beth's heart. But she ignored the wistful stab of longing. Perhaps because she was unable to decide if the pang was because of all *she* had missed as a child or because she was pretty sure she didn't have what it took to be a parent.

A request for a refill pulled her back to the present. It was clear that people in this room were dealing with a host of emotions. Obviously, they were grateful for the meal and the shelter. But many of the men and women gathered under this one big roof were unaccustomed to accepting handouts. They seemed shell-shocked, as if still not quite believing they had lost their homes and most of their possessions.

Beth had an advantage there. She had learned at an early age that *things* could be taken away. One dismal January when the rent was due and money was nonexistent, Beth's mother had done the unthinkable: she pawned the two shiny new bicycles a charity group had provided for Beth and Audie at Christmas. Audie wailed, but Beth never shed a tear, her grief and anger too deep to articulate. From then on, she understood that happiness was not to be trusted if it depended on accumulating material belongings.

She liked nice things. But she wasn't driven to purchase them for herself. It was far more satisfying to put time and effort into her fields and to watch new life grow. Her house had been ripped apart, and there was a good chance that her brother would rob her blind. But she had to let it go. Those realities were out of her control.

In the end, Audie could only hurt her if she valued what he took. She had no childhood mementos. No much-loved antiques that had been her grandmother's. No school trophies. No heirloom jewelry.

All she had was herself and her determination to make a good life. A clean life. A life worth living. It was a truth she shared with many in this room.

When the last of the refugees had been served, Beth and her co-workers sat down to eat. Drew snagged the seat beside her at the last minute. They ate quickly. It had been a long time since lunch.

Beneath the table, his thigh pressed against hers. The chairs were crunched closely together because of the confined space. It was impossible to ignore him even if she had wanted to.

He reached over and used his napkin to wipe a dab of sauce from her chin. "You about ready to go home?"

She nodded, feeling breathless suddenly. Drew's gaze was warm and intimate. Did he mean for the evening to conclude in a very special way? They were both dirty and sweaty. Nothing in their current situation could be construed as romantic by any stretch of the imagination. But when his hand brushed hers, her throat constricted and her body felt hot and achy.

For months she had seen him as an adversary. A very sexy, gorgeous man, but someone to keep at bay, nevertheless. Now, the lines were blurred. They had shared a terrifying experience. Not only that, but they were working side by side in the town they both loved.

Comrades in arms often developed deep friendships during time spent in battle. Beth and Drew found themselves serving in the trenches, as it were. Their physical closeness had accelerated the formation of a definite bond. But as much as she liked and respected Drew, she definitely wanted more than friendship.

Wanting was okay. Crossing a physical line was okay. As long as she understood he wasn't hers to keep.

Drew was bone tired and yet still aroused. He admired Beth so much. Despite personal losses, she had plunged headfirst into helping her neighbors. Instead of fretting about her own disaster, she acted as if nothing were wrong.

On the way back to the ranch, he glanced at his silent partner. "Do you want to stop by your house and check on things?"

"No." She didn't dress up her refusal.

"Are you sure? It won't take but a minute."

"I said no."

The snap in her voice pissed him off. He could have found any one of a number of topics to chat about, but her stubbornness shut him up. Surely her brother's situation weighed on her. It was easily within Drew's power to erase all that stress. He had a legitimate job available for Audie. If Beth had asked, Drew would even move Audie and his family to Willowbrook temporarily.

So either Beth didn't *want* to help her brother, or Beth didn't want to accept Drew's help. Come to think about it, she hadn't exactly been enthused about staying at Willowbrook Farms herself.

Pulling up in front of the home where he had lived since birth, Drew shoved the gearshift into park, got out, and slammed the door. Hard. If Beth didn't want his assistance, he wouldn't force it on her. He had better things to do than wrangle with a hardheaded woman.

He unlocked the front door, not waiting to see if she had followed him. The house echoed with emptiness. The housekeeper had gone home, as had all of Drew's staff except for the handful of guys who kept watch over the animals at night. Now he and Beth were alone. The thought tormented him.

He went straight to his bedroom, stripped off his filthy clothes and stalked toward the shower. The erection rearing thick and hungry against his belly made him grit his teeth. How in the hell could he want a woman so badly and at the same time feel the urge to shake her until her teeth rattled?

Usually he appreciated the luxury of triple showerheads. Tonight, the marble enclosure made him feel isolated and alone. That simple realization shook him. Since when did he *need* a woman? For sex, sure. He understood that drive. But the burning in his gut was about more than getting laid. He thought he and Beth had made progress toward becoming friends. Apparently, he was wrong.

He was so wound up in his righteous indignation that he didn't notice at first when the glass door opened.

"Need some company?"

He whirled around so fast his feet nearly slid out from under him. That would have topped it all. Ending up assfirst, naked and wet at her feet.

"Beth…." He eased off on the hot water. Steam made it difficult for him to see, and he definitely didn't want to miss a moment. "What are you doing here?"

It was a stupid question. Even he admitted that. She was wearing her shirt from today. And nothing else. The hem of the rumpled garment ended at the top of long, shapely legs. She had taken her hair down. Her toes curled against the stone floor, so maybe she wasn't quite as blasé as she wanted to appear.

"We started something earlier," she said. "At the school. I'm sorry I ruined the mood by arguing with you."

Some mysterious constriction in his chest eased. He

picked up a curl that lay on her shoulder. "So soft," he muttered.

"Do you still want me?"

"Oh, yes." Slowly, he unbuttoned her top. She'd had the foresight to remove her bra already. Soon nothing stood between him and the lush female flesh waiting to be touched, stroked, mapped with every hill and valley noted.

Beth seemed frozen, barely breathing. She watched him, eyes downcast, as he traced her collarbone, played lightly with her tight nipples, lifted and plumped her soft breasts. He was trying his damnedest to go slow. But when she closed her eyes and shuddered, he almost lost it.

Gently, he tugged at the cotton shirt until it slid down her arms. He pulled it free and tossed it out of the shower. "Come inside," he said hoarsely. "We're getting the bathroom floor wet."

His prosaic request sounded awkward to his ears. But coherent speech was difficult if not impossible. All the blood in his body had run south, leaving him lightheaded and perilously lost to reason.

Beth looked up at him. She laid a hand, palm flat, against his stubbly cheek. "Will you wash my hair?" she asked. Her big shadowy eyes held secrets...feminine wiles. She was so close to him their thighs brushed. His sex throbbed against her belly, eager to see action.

"Of course," he said gruffly. "Turn around."

Her creamy skin was flawless. Until now, he had never realized that shoulder blades could be sexy. But when they pointed the way to a nipped-in waist and a butt shaped to fit a man's hands, the view was mouthwatering. He kissed the nape of her neck before reaching for a plastic bottle. His shampoo was scented with pine. He had a feeling that from tonight forward, this particular smell was going to provoke a Pavlovian response.

Easing her backward a step, he covered her eyes with his hand and directed the stream of water until it darkened and straightened her thick, vibrant hair. When every strand was soaked, he adjusted the spray in the opposite direction and pulled her flush against him until her bottom nestled in the cradle of his thighs.

It was a very perverse form of self-torture, but things got worse when he began rubbing soapy liquid into her hair. His fingers caressed her scalp. Beth groaned—a sexy, visceral sound that tightened every muscle in his body despite the warm shower. It was the most effective form of foreplay he had ever tried.

Beth seemed to be enjoying it, but more to the point, the gentle massage actually sent *his* libido into a state of high alert. He reached around her with both arms and slid his hands across slick breasts. Was *she* panting, or was it he?

It occurred to him—despite his mental faculties being sluggish—that the sooner he finished this project, the sooner he'd have Beth in his bed where he wanted her. Exercising admirable control, he returned to the task at hand and began rinsing her hair. Tiny soap bubbles clung to his fingers, even as strands of dark gold wound themselves around his wrists.

Beth remained silent. Since he was behind her, he couldn't see her expression. Finally, after interminable minutes, he decided his job was complete. He had to clear his throat to speak. "All done," he said.

She turned slowly, her lips curved in a smile of feminine amusement. "You have hidden talents, Mr. Farrell."

"I'm only getting started."

"That's nice to know." The air that surrounded them was thick with moisture and charged with anticipation.

Without asking for permission, she reached for the soap and a washcloth. Something about the lazy movements of her hands as she rubbed the plain white bar against the navy cotton square mesmerized him. "I think I was already clean before you joined me," he pointed out, eager to move things along.

Beth reached up to kiss him, her lips clinging just long enough to drive him insane.

"I should make sure you didn't miss any spots," she whispered. "Put your hands behind your neck and spread your legs."

He obeyed instinctively. Compliance was a foregone conclusion.

Without realizing it, he closed his eyes. When Beth touched him on the upper thigh, he flinched...hard. Her husky laugh sent desire raging through his veins. "Hell, Beth. Warn a guy, why don't you?"

Warm, rough strokes were her answer. Somehow she managed to avoid his erection. She dragged the wet, soapy cloth over and around his thighs and between his legs. His teeth dug so hard into his lower lip he tasted the tang of blood.

"Enough," he groaned.

"If you say so." She aimed the water at his abdomen, creating a waterfall that cascaded down his groin. In some dim, barely reasoning corner of his brain, he registered the fact that his next water bill was going to be outrageous.

Without warning, slender fingers closed around his shaft. *Holy hell.* He was so close to coming that his vision blurred.

With her free hand, she stroked his chest. "Don't fight it, Drew," she whispered. "Let go. Enjoy."

He grabbed her close, clutching her against him as he came with an audible groan that encompassed shock, amazement and physical nirvana.

* * *

Beth scarcely knew herself. It had taken great courage to invade Drew's privacy impetuously. But earlier today, they had turned up the heat. The wanting and needing had remained on a slow boil all afternoon and evening. It was only her stubbornness that had caused the rift.

Drew wanted to do everything he could for her. He was generous to a fault. And even Beth acknowledged that providing assistance to those in need should not always be predicated on whether or not the recipient *deserved* the help.

But Audie was a different story. Beth had been burned too many times in the past to believe that her brother had really changed. She loathed the idea of Drew taking a peek into her life, her gene pool. How could he look at Audie and *not* make some judgments about Beth, even if they were unconscious?

Since she didn't want to get into complicated explanations of why she wanted to keep Drew far away from her brother, she did the next best thing. She let Drew see how much she wanted him, and how far she was willing to go.

Even in the aftermath of an impressive orgasm, he was quick on the uptake. He hustled them both out of the shower and made her stand still while he dried her from head to toe with a thick towel. Remaining passive beneath his touch was no hardship. His gentle care was at once soothing and arousing.

"Open your eyes, Beth."

She obeyed reluctantly, fearing what she might see on his face. Taking the lead in sex the way she had in the shower was not her M.O. Some men would not like the tables being turned. It was programmed into male DNA to be the pursuer.

Drew stared at her, his eyes glittering with unveiled

hunger. "I applaud your inventive enthusiasm, but this next time I'm not leaving you behind."

"I can live with that."

He scooped her into his arms and carried her into his bedroom. She had been so nervous going into this that his masculine domain had barely registered. Now, particularly after he turned on a small lamp on the chest, she saw a room that was both elegant and comfortable.

The navy carpet alone was hedonistic. Thick and soft, it invited toes to flex in its luxury. The bed was massive, a dark mahogany four-poster king covered in ivory damask. There was nothing remotely feminine about the decorating scheme, but Beth fell in love with the ambiance.

Drew appeared to hesitate for a moment. She looked up at him. "Is there a problem?"

His lips curled in a smile that sent shivers down her spine. "Not at all. I was merely counting up how many times and ways I want to take you and where to start."

Her mouth dried. Feverish and needy, she raked her fingernails across his shoulder. "Swear you mean that."

"Every word."

Dumping her on her feet without ceremony, he threw back the covers and ripped open a drawer in the bedside table to find protection. The handful of packets he dropped on the tabletop was impressive.

He crooked a finger, his flash of white teeth wicked. "It's your turn now, little tease. Prepare to be ravished."

Without protest, she allowed him to draw her toward a mattress that seemed a mile wide. She shrieked when he lifted her without warning and tossed her onto soft sheets. Scrambling to appear worldly rather than awkward and ungainly, she curled on her side and pulled a corner of the sheet over her.

With one quick jerk of his hand, her modesty was history. "Don't hide from me, Beth."

"I wasn't."

His knowing smile acknowledged her lie. "Put your hands behind your neck and spread your legs."

Somehow, when Drew repeated the command she had spoken to him in the shower, the words took on a whole new meaning. She melted from the inside out, every muscle in her body turning to heat and energy.

He watched with hooded eyes as she forced herself to comply. Deliberately exposing her sex to his hungry gaze took more courage than it had to invade his shower. "Be gentle with me," she joked, jittery with nervous anticipation.

"The first time."

Wow. How could a man infuse three syllables with such delicious intent and promise? She sucked in a deep breath and exhaled as he lowered himself next to her, his body radiating heat. "Why have we waited so long to do this?" he asked, teasing her navel with a fingertip.

She writhed and panted. "Because I'm a thorn in your side."

"I can't remember why." He bent his head and kissed her flat tummy.

"That's because you're not thinking with the correct portion of your anatomy."

"Damned straight. We're in the midst of a truce. So I propose that you stay in my bed for as many hours as it takes for us both to get tired of each other."

"How long will that be?"

He parted the folds of her sex with his thumbs. Her back arched instinctively.

"I'll let you know," he muttered.

After that, conversation halted in favor of sheer, carnal

pleasure. Drew's expertise was unmistakable. He touched her reverently, like a man examining a newfound treasure.

When she wanted him to go fast, he slowed down. When she craved more pressure, he gave her butterfly caresses. Pleasure built. Wanting multiplied. Her climax hit with the force of a thunderstorm, drenching her with delirium.

She reached for him. "Drew. Drew...."

He did what had to be done and moved between her legs, sliding his hands beneath her thighs and opening her even further to his possession. Feeling the blunt head of his sex as he pushed into her was in some ways more frightening than the tornado. How could she survive this? She had been halfway in love with him for months, disguising her silly unrequited crush as indifference.

Apparently, one of the reasons she had argued with him about her produce stand and her customers was to keep him coming back again and again. How pathetic was that? She'd lied to herself and not even seen the truth. If it had not already been far too late for second thoughts, she might have run from the room. With every stroke of his body inside hers, he left his imprint. She would never be the same.

But as he loved her slowly and tenderly, fear gave way to wonder and hesitation became assurance. Nothing so wonderful could be a mistake. She gave herself up to the deep, drugged pleasure of his lovemaking.

Muscles bunched in his arms as he struggled to keep his weight off her. "Tell me you won't regret this," he demanded.

"I came to you, remember?"

"Doesn't matter. I see your eyes. You're already running scared."

His perspicacity embarrassed her. She couldn't deny the truth.

So she arched her back, driving him a fraction deeper,

clenching his hard length with inner muscles. "I'm here now. Don't stop, Drew. Please." She teetered on the brink of a spectacular finish.

His answer was to give her everything she wanted. No more nuances. No more time for talk. He was big and hard and determined to push her off the ledge. "Come for me, darlin'," he muttered.

She did as he asked, but only because she had no choice. If she had ever experienced such pure, crystalline pleasure, she couldn't remember it. The ripples went on and on, leaving her breathless and lost.

Drew was seconds behind her, his climax signaled by a harsh shout and thrusting hips. With her legs wrapped around his waist, Beth clung to his wide shoulders and held on as her universe tumbled out of control.

Nine

Drew lay perfectly still, waiting for his thundering heart-beat to return to a normal cadence. Beth had fallen asleep immediately, worn out by their long day and his crazed lovemaking. As promised, he had taken her more than once—the second time sitting in an armchair with Beth straddling his lap, and finally, bending her over the foot of the bed and making the last coupling slow and sweet.

By all rights, he should be exhausted as well. But adrenaline pumped through his veins. Being with Beth tonight had been far more than physically gratifying. The connection they forged had opened his eyes to what was missing in his life. Falling in love with a woman had been something for the future…the kind of thing a man did when he was ready to settle down.

Apparently, unbeknownst to him, love had grown in spite of his self-deception. As incredible as it seemed, his frequent trips to Beth's place of business had been about far more than her patrons spooking his horses.

He had been irresistibly drawn to her spirit and her beauty. The storm's wrath had ripped away wood and metal and shingles, but it had also laid bare an astonishing truth. Drew Farrell had feelings for Beth Andrews. Deep, messy emotions.

Her head lay pillowed on his shoulder. He combed her

curls with one hand as contentment slid through his veins like honey. Tomorrow she would probably fuss about how her hair looked because she had not dried it. But Drew liked the wild tangle. It was a reflection of the intimacy they had shared.

She had let down her guard with him tonight. For a woman so fiercely independent, he understood very well what a gift she offered. They had met as equals and by her choice. What he didn't know was the outcome of tonight's excess.

Tomorrow would be the test. Would he see the real Beth, or would the walls be up once again?

Beth awoke at first light, disoriented, but very relaxed. It took a handful of seconds for reality to come crashing in. Drew's room. Drew's bed. Drew's big, muscular body wrapped around hers.

What have I done?

The wanting had been building for over a year. No surprises there. But why had she acted on it? Why now?

She could tell herself it was because of the storm or because she was staying in Drew's house or even because she was lonely and displaced. But the truth was far simpler. Yesterday, she had felt the relentless pull of sexual need, and she had given in. Not only that, she had wallowed in it without shame or regret.

The truth was shocking but impossible to ignore.

Gingerly, she lifted his heavy arm and scooted away from him. He stirred, grumbling, but buried his face in his pillow and continued to sleep.

Fortunately, gathering her things was not an issue. One shirt. That was it. One shirt to protect her modesty as she scuttled back to her room. She had no idea how early the household staff arrived, but surely not at this hour.

When she made it without incident to the relative safety of her own suite, she debated what to do. It would probably be a good idea to wet her hair and dry it again before getting dressed. But a yawn caught her by surprise. It had been a harrowing three days. Removing her one item of clothing, she tossed back the covers on the decadently luxurious bed and climbed naked beneath the sheets.

It was a warm autumn in Texas, but the crisp cotton felt chilled after snuggling with Drew all night. Her body was pleasurably sore as she settled into a comfy spot. Remembering Drew's attentions was not a good idea. After a long hiatus, her libido was alive and well.

Closing her eyes, she gave herself over to the numbing drug of sleep. She had acted rashly, impulsively, totally without forethought. The results had been amazing, but it was time to retreat and regroup.

She knew now what it was like to be with Drew. It was good. Really good. Before she got in too deeply, she had to set some ground rules for herself. Drew's amicability was only temporary. When she was living in her house again, they would revert to the same impasse. Drew had the time and the money and the determination to badger her until she gave in to his wishes. Plus, the storm had weakened her resolve and her certainty about the farm as her life's work.

Equally depressing was the fact that Audie would always be a millstone around her neck. She came from questionable roots. Everyone in the horse business knew that breeding was everything.

Even if a tornado had thrown Beth and Drew together—literally—they had nothing in common but sharing a frightening ordeal. That wasn't enough on which to build a relationship.

After an hour of tossing and turning, she gave up and

got out of bed. Perhaps a hot shower would settle her jangled emotions. The prospect of coming face to face with Drew made her ridiculously nervous. What would she say to him?

She dressed in a pair of faded jeans and a comfortable sky blue polo shirt. No need to make a good impression. There was work to be done.

After a quick call to her insurance agent to follow up on Allen's report, she went in search of breakfast. If she were lucky, Drew would be somewhere out on the ranch tending to business. The thought of a hot cup of coffee with a side of morning solitude was irresistible.

Unfortunately, only half of her order was on the menu. When she entered the kitchen, she pulled up short, dismayed to find it full of people, or so it seemed. Though the housekeeper excused herself to go tend to the laundry, the kitchen table was occupied. Drew and Jed and a woman who looked strangely familiar were helping themselves to bacon and sausage and eggs as well as pancakes and grapefruit.

"Sorry to intrude," she said quietly. "I'll just grab a cup of coffee."

Drew stood up and pulled out a chair. "Don't be silly. Join us." The look in his eyes dared her to disagree.

With her cheeks warm and her legs quivering, she sank into the chair and tried not to flinch when Drew's hand brushed her shoulder. Had the motion been deliberate? The last thing in the world she had expected or wanted was an audience for their inescapable morning after.

Jed touched the woman's arm. "Kimberly, this is Beth Andrews. Her house was damaged by the tornado, so she's staying here at Willowbrook for a bit."

The brunette smiled. "I know who you are, but you probably don't remember me. I came to Green Acres several times last summer to buy vegetables. Your heirloom tomatoes were so good."

"Thank you," Beth said. "And yes, I do remember you now. You used to come into the bank when I was working there…you made deposits for the dress shop."

"Yes, I did."

"So," Drew said, changing the subject and lifting an eyebrow as he stared at his brother. "I'm always glad to have guests for breakfast, but I'm sensing your visit has a particular agenda."

Jed looked at Kimberly. She motioned for him to do the honors. Jed took her hand and faced his brother. "Kimberly and I are going to get married." After noting the shocked silence from Drew and Beth, he continued. "We had planned to do something quick and easy at the courthouse, but obviously that's out of the question. And we're not sure it's appropriate to have a marriage ceremony at all with so many people suffering."

Jed and Kimberly sat shoulder to shoulder, their fingers entwined. Between them shimmered an almost palpable tenderness. Beth couldn't help but feel a twinge of envy. Jed looked at Kimberly as if she were the answer to all his prayers wrapped up in one lovely package.

Drew cleared his throat, obviously emotional about his younger brother getting hitched. "Congratulations, you two."

Beth nodded and smiled. "And from me as well. But I have to say, I think a wedding might be the perfect occasion to bring some joy and cheer to what have been pretty bleak days in Royal."

"You could have the ceremony here," Drew said. "We'll invite all our friends."

"I'd be honored to help any way I can," Beth said. "Though to be honest, I don't know much about planning an event like that. But I am pretty organized if that counts for anything."

Kimberly's smile held gratitude. "You're both being very sweet about this, but the thing is…" She trailed off, biting her lip.

Jed picked up where she left off. "The thing is…an affair like that takes time to put together."

Drew frowned. "What's the rush, Jed? Can't Dallas do without you for another six or eight weeks? You could fly back and forth if you needed to."

Jed's cheekbones flushed with color. The look he gave Kimberly was so fiercely and intimately personal, Beth felt as if she were witnessing something very private.

"Go on," Kimberly whispered, her cheeks rosy as well. She gazed at Jed with starry-eyed adoration.

Jed kissed her gently on the cheek before turning back to his brother. "Kimberly and I are going to have a baby. In about six months."

Beth had seldom seen Drew speechless, but he couldn't have looked any more surprised if someone had whacked him over the head with a two by four. "A baby? Why didn't you tell me before now?"

Jed and Kimberly exchanged wry glances. "I only found out myself right before the storm hit. I had just asked her to marry me when all hell broke loose."

Beth laughed softly. "That must have been some proposal."

Drew stood up and tugged his brother and Kimberly to their feet, hugging them fiercely. "I'm damned happy and excited for the both of you." He kissed Kimberly's cheek gently. "Welcome to the family. Jed's a lucky man."

After that, the conversation escalated, everyone talking at once and making plans. Beth glanced at her watch.

"Oh, shoot. I've got to run. I promised Megan that I'd help her again today."

Drew's brows drew together as he frowned. "I'll take you."

Beth stood her ground. She needed a little personal space. It was hard to be rational with Drew in touching distance. "It will be better for me to drive myself," she said. "I don't know how long I'll be there. And besides, the three of you have lots to talk about. I'll be back by suppertime."

She cut and ran before he could argue. With his brother and soon to be sister-in-law in his kitchen, he couldn't very well chase after her.

By the time she reached the shelter, she had made a firm decision not to think about Drew for the rest of the day. It was a good goal if she could stick to it.

Megan was delighted to see her. "Beth, you're wonderful to come help when you have your own problems. How are things going with your house?"

"Believe it or not, and thanks to Drew who got me in with a building inspector, it looks like I may have a check in hand by the middle of next week. Now all I have to do is line up a contractor."

"You two are being awfully chummy considering your history. Couldn't you ask Drew to help with that, too?"

Beth shook her head. "I'm sure he *could,* but I'm not going to let him. I'm a grown woman. My house is my responsibility. Besides, he—" She stopped short, realizing that Jed and Kimberly might not want their business blabbed all over the county.

Megan cocked her head, her arms full of wriggling kittens. "He what?"

"You have to promise me you won't say anything. I don't know if this news is ready to go public yet."

The other woman mimed locking her lips. "I'll take it to my grave."

"Drew's brother Jed is getting married. To Kimberly Fanning. And the wedding will be at Willowbrook, I think. Drew is going to be plenty busy without me playing the helpless female."

"That's exciting. But I'm sure no one looks at you as a helpless *anything,* Beth. Look at how you started your farm from scratch."

"Well, the tornado took care of that. I'll bet my pumpkins ended up smashed to bits all over the county."

"At least you can joke about it."

Beth shrugged. "I'm one of the lucky ones. I wasn't injured, and my house is not a total loss. I can't complain."

"You certainly have a great attitude about all of this. I suppose it helps to have a handsome rancher in your back pocket."

"I told you before. Drew is only being kind." The excuse was not quite as easy to stand behind today. Not with everything that had happened in Drew's bed last night. She felt her cheeks heat. Her vow not to think about the sexy billionaire was shot already, which didn't say much about her willpower.

Megan deposited the kittens in front of a large bowl of milk and touched Beth's arm. "Your new friend has been waiting for you." She pointed to a cage nearby.

"Oh, Stormy." Beth's heart melted. The little dog looked healthy, but his mournful eyes seemed to say he had hoped Beth would come back. She unlocked the mesh door and scooped him up for a hug. "I didn't forget about you, I swear. You are the sweetest thing."

Stormy burrowed closer with a bark of happiness.

Megan grinned. "He knows a soft touch when he sees one."

"Has anyone asked about him?"

"No. I traced the number on his collar and spoke with his owner. Turns out they dumped him on my doorstep because they couldn't afford dog food anymore. Stormy is an orphan."

"What is his real name?"

"Do you honestly want to know? Or would you rather think of him as Stormy?"

"Good point. Will it confuse him if I call him that?"

Megan laughed. "As long as you agree to be his mama, I think he'll let you do anything you want."

Drew was happy for his brother and Kimberly. He really was. But a man had a finite amount of patience for wedding details—unless of course, it was his own woman bubbling over with joy. With one ear he listened to Jed make suggestions to his newly-minted fiancée about ways to use the elegance of Willowbrook Farms for a romantic occasion. Even keeping things simple, the timetable would be a challenge.

Drew chimed in when appropriate, but in truth, all he could think about was Beth. Wet and willing in his shower. Naked and naughty in his bed. Limber and luscious in any number of heart-pounding scenarios. The previous night was etched in his memory. Probably forever. He knew they were attracted to each other. What he hadn't expected was the feelings that went beyond the physical.

The raw need and urgent passion Beth stirred in his gut alarmed him. It had been a long time since a sexual encounter turned him inside out. He'd felt invincible.

But when he woke up this morning, Beth was gone. He told himself there was no need to jump to conclusions. Maybe she was bashful about rehashing their experience

in the cold light of day…or perhaps embarrassed that someone might see her come out of his room.

Or maybe it hadn't been good for her.

He refused to believe that. Beth had been like sunshine in his arms…passionate, teasing, warming him in
every way possible. When he showered this morning, his
body had reminded him painfully of last night's excess.
His sex hardened as he remembered the feel of her hands
on his body.

Instead of hunting her down in her room, he'd done
the gentlemanly thing and waited for her in the kitchen.
Then all his plans had gone awry when Jed and Kimberly
showed up. Drew had not had a single opportunity to talk
privately with Beth. In fact, she'd barely made eye contact with him.

And now she was gone for the day. He could drop by
the shelter again, but he had no real excuse for doing so.
He'd never lacked confidence when it came to women. But
he'd rather not have witnesses to a post-coital confrontation that might not turn out the way he hoped.

He glanced at his watch and stood up. "You two love-
birds stay as long as you want. But I promised to help at
the courthouse today. They're trying to recover as many
documents as possible before it rains again. I may try to
speak to Colby Richardson, too. Offer my sympathies.
He's come back to town to bury his brother, Craig, and to
be supportive of Craig's widow, Paige. That and dealing
with the ranch will be a lot for one man to handle."

Jed nodded. "Yeah, it will. I'm supposed to work a shift
later. I'll see you down there."

Drew hugged Kimberly, stunned to realize that the
thought of being an uncle was pretty damned exciting.
"Welcome to the family."

* * *

As Drew neared the turn to Green Acres, he pondered Beth's attitude toward Audie. *Forget about my brother.* Surely she didn't really mean that. He turned his truck onto Beth's road, calling himself all kinds of a fool. But try as he might, he couldn't ignore the fact that Audie needed a job and Drew could help. Surely that would ease some of Beth's emotional burden. She didn't need to be worrying about her brother in addition to everything else she was juggling.

The house looked much the same. Fortunately, the moderate temperatures had continued, so no one was in any danger of freezing to death, even if the shed wasn't heated. Audie sat on a tree stump smoking. He didn't move when Drew put the vehicle in park and got out.

Drew lifted a hand. "Thought I'd stop by and check on you."

Audie's nodded. "Where's sis?"

"Helping out at the animal shelter. I'm sure she'll see you later."

"Wouldn't count on it." Audie paused to flick a mosquito off his knee. "Can I help you with something?"

"Actually, I might be able to help you. One of my stable hands quit last week, so I have a job available. It's not glamorous work. The pay is decent but not great. But since you're staying here, you could save up a deposit for another place in town."

"Does Beth know you're here?"

A warning flag went up. "No. This is between us."

"She won't like it. She doesn't believe I've really changed."

"Changed how?"

"I've been a drunk most of my life. But I finally started

going to AA, and now I've been sober for six months. My history is why I've had trouble getting a job."

"How bad is it?"

Audie shrugged. "I've had a few run-ins with the law. Nothing major. I had to clean up my act when the baby came along."

"We run a tight ship at Willowbrook. You would be answering to my manager. I'm doing this for your sister, but I expect a lot from my men."

"I hear what you're saying."

"In that case, do you want the job?"

Audie took off a stained baseball cap and scratched his head. "I don't much like gettin' up early."

Drew winced inwardly. He was beginning to see why Beth had issues with Audie. "The job is 7:30 to 4:00 with half an hour for lunch and two fifteen minute breaks. No smoking anywhere on the property."

"Okay. I guess I can live with that. I appreciate you taking a chance on me."

"Let me be straight with you, Audie. I could have a dozen guys lining up for the chance to work at Willowbrook. My stable hands are the best in the business. You'll learn a lot from them. The only reason I'm offering you this job is because I care about your sister."

Audie nodded. "I bet you do."

Drew inhaled sharply. With two hands, he took Audie by the collar and lifted him to his toes— wishing he could put his hands around his neck.

Audie went the color of skim milk when Drew got in his face and snarled, "You will *not* disrespect your sister. Are we clear?" When the man nodded, Drew released him, chest heaving.

Beth's skinny sibling got to his feet, grabbed up his dust-covered ball cap, and had the audacity to ask for more.

"I'll need a way to get to work. Can't leave the wife and kid without a car."

This time Drew had to count to ten. "One of my guys passes here every morning. I'll see if he's willing to pick you up. Now do you want the job or not?"

"Yeah. I appreciate it. I really do. But Beth may get her feathers ruffled. She's not big on taking help."

"Are you the only family she has? I know your parents are gone. But no aunts and uncles? Cousins?"

"Wouldn't know on my dad's side. Mama was an only child. Me and Beth aren't bosom buddies. She's a little uppity. Thinks she's better than me."

"I warned you."

Audie took two steps backward. "I gotta check on things."

"You'll be ready in the morning?"

"Yup."

"Don't waste this opportunity."

"I won't, Mr. Farrell. You won't be sorry."

Ten

Drew brooded about the unsettling encounter with Beth's brother all the way into town. No wonder Beth had warned him off. Audie's reinvention of himself might or might not be the real deal. Only time would tell. But Drew was determined to insert himself between Beth and the stress of looking after her brother. She didn't need to worry about Audie and his family if Drew was around to help. It was the least Drew could do.

In Royal, reality hit once again. Sifting through the wreckage of Town Hall was a distraction, but not a welcome one. Knowing people had lost their lives on this very spot was sobering. A pall of tragedy lay over the site. Though at least two dozen volunteers worked side by side in an attempt to recover valuable records, there was no joking, no camaraderie. Faces were grim. Eyes were shadowed with grief.

Lord knew how anything would ever get back to normal.

In the midst of the backbreaking work, once again Drew realized how lucky he and Beth had been. Imagining her snatched from his side by a killer tornado made him queasy. And it could have happened. So easily....

Today, the skies above were innocent and blue, nothing at all like what he remembered from the day of the storm. He had a feeling that many in Royal would experience post-traumatic stress in the weeks and months to come. Thankfully, the calendar said they were on the tail end of tornado season, but next spring would be another story. Every thunderstorm promised to be nerve-wracking, especially for the children who didn't really understand these things.

Pausing to take a swig of water, he noticed a piece of paper flapping in the breeze, anchored by a chunk of concrete block. He squatted to pick it up and saw that it was a fragment of a marriage license. Neither of the names was familiar to him. But for a moment, he was struck by how many people would be affected by this mess at Town Hall. Were any of the computer records recoverable?

After his long, difficult shift wrapped up, he acknowledged he wasn't going to have any peace of mind until he had it out with Beth. He was hot and tired and second-guessing himself about getting involved with Audie. Sooner or later he would have to confess to Beth what he had done. His job offer had been motivated by a desire to help Beth, perhaps even to earn her gratitude. But he was coming to realize that she didn't always see things the way Drew did. He would postpone that hurdle for as long as possible.

Cell service was pretty good now. He thought about calling or texting, but instead, he drove over to the shelter, arriving just as Beth walked out the front door. She didn't notice him at first. Her head was bent as she talked softly to a little bundle of caramel-colored fur.

Drew closed the distance between them. "I remember that little fellow. What's his name?"

Beth halted abruptly, seeming startled but pleased to see him. "I call him Stormy. It turns out his owners abandoned him the other day. I may adopt him as soon as my house is finished."

"Lucky dog." He toyed with the puppy's ear. "We need to talk about last night."

Beth's cheeks turned pink. "Lower your voice, for Pete's sake. And if you mean the sex—" She stopped abruptly.

He smoothed her hair behind her ear. She hadn't worn it up this time. The long gold waves danced in the breeze. "What *about* the sex?"

Her head ducked as she focused all her interest on the dog. "It was good."

"Good? That's it? Not much of an affirmation."

"What do you want from me, Drew?" She shot him a sideways glance that told him she wasn't accustomed to discussing her sex life so matter-of-factly.

Come to think of it, neither was he. But he wanted to be sure that last night was not a one-time thing. "I've thought about you all day," he murmured, thankful that Megan was not in earshot. "I was disappointed to wake up and find you gone."

"I wasn't thinking very clearly. I didn't want to make a mistake."

"And did you?"

At last she raised her chin. Squaring her shoulders, she met his gaze full on, her smile small but genuine. "I'll let you know."

He shook his head with a rueful grin, glancing at his watch. "You're a hard woman, Beth Andrews." Her stubbornness worried him on another count. Drew planned to tell her he had hired Audie. And to explain that his intention in doing so was to make life easier for Beth...because he cared about her.

But her pride and her aversion to taking help might be Drew's downfall. This *thing* between the two of them was fragile. Before confessing, he had to be sure she wanted him enough to overlook the fact that he had gone behind her back.

"I came by with a proposition," he said. "How would you feel about a quick trip to Dallas?"

"Don't we have plenty to do here?"

"Of course we do. But Jed is supposed to be present at a meeting tomorrow morning at his headquarters. He doesn't want to leave Kimberly right now, so I said I would take his place since I sit on his board. If you come along, we can spend the night, have a nice dinner, take a break from all of this."

"I don't have anything to wear."

"I thought you might say that. Kimberly works at a clothing store in town."

"A very high-end establishment," Beth said wryly. "Not my price range at all."

"She's already picked out several outfits with her discount. You can return any you don't like."

"Has anyone ever told you how bossy you are?"

"It might have come up." He kissed her cheek. "C'mon, Beth. Say yes."

"Isn't it a little late to be booking a flight?"

"I have a helicopter."

Well, of course you do. Beth gaped, although why she was surprised, she didn't know. Drew was an incredibly wealthy man. "I see." She wrinkled her nose, deciding how honest she was willing to be. "After the tornado, I'm not sure I'm up for riding in anything that whirls in the sky."

Drew chuckled. "My pilot is one of the best. You have nothing to worry about."

Except being wined and dined and treated like a queen and falling in love with the king. That kind of stuff could go to a girl's head. "Okay. But I've never flown before, so if I freak out, it's all your fault."

He wrapped his arms around her from behind and nuzzled her ear. "I'll take care of you, Beth. I swear."

He was warm and tall, and his hard, muscled arms folded her close. Instinctively, she leaned into him, her back against his chest. Her heart began to jump and race. Stormy wriggled in her arms, ready to get down and play. Beth swallowed hard. "I should see if Megan needs anything else."

Drew nipped her earlobe. "Come home with me, now. Kimberly promised to have the dresses at the ranch by dinnertime. She and Jed are going to eat with us. After that, I'm planning on an early night."

Beth peeked over her shoulder, their lips almost touching. "Because you're exhausted from working all day?"

Drew's eyes flashed with barely concealed hunger. His jaw, covered in dark stubble, was carved in granite. Clearly, he hadn't shaved that morning. "I could be comatose," he said gruffly, "and I would still want you in my bed. But don't count on getting much sleep. You can nap at the hotel tomorrow while I go to the meeting."

An odd lethargy stole through Beth's muscles, making her limbs weak. He smelled of sweat and warm male. Not a combination she'd ever found erotic before now. But then again, Drew Farrell was one of a kind.

"Let me tell Megan I'm leaving," she whispered, ruefully aware that his sexuality drew her despite her determination to establish boundaries. She didn't even *want* to resist. Not anymore.

Drew waited in his truck with the engine running while she said her goodbyes and tucked Stormy back into his cage. The puppy settled onto his soft, warm blanket and rested his chin on his paws, regarding her with mournful eyes.

"Don't give me that look," she said, laughing at the small animal's innate ability to make her feel guilty. "You're going to live with me. But not yet."

With one quick word to Megan, who was struggling to coax a large Labrador into eating unfamiliar food, Beth grabbed her purse and her water bottle and ran outside. Drew's impatience was palpable.

Grinning to herself—equally eager for the night ahead—she pulled in behind him and followed him back to the ranch.

An hour later, standing in the beautiful bedroom Drew had given her, Beth stared at herself in the mirror and bit her lip. "I don't know, Kimberly. Isn't it a little...um... skimpy?"

Kimberly laughed, handing her a mist-gray shawl that was soft as a butterfly wing. "The dress is perfect. It showcases your assets."

If by assets the other woman meant breasts, then yes. No question there. The black cocktail dress dipped low in the front and even lower in the back. The silk and jersey blend clung to every curve of Beth's body as if it had been sewn onto her. Narrow rhinestone straps were its only embellishment.

"This must be horribly expensive," she said. How could she justify purchasing anything so frivolous and impractical when her house was partially demolished? She was playing dress-up with a man who was way out of her league.

"I'm giving you my discount. You can afford all of this stuff and not break the bank." Kimberly obviously picked up on Beth's ambivalence. She shook her head and folded her arms across her chest. "I think I know what's going on. You have a thing for Drew, but you don't want to get hurt."

"You have to admit that we're an unlikely couple. His prize thoroughbreds have a better lineage than I do."

Kimberly took her arm and steered her toward a chair, forcing her to sit. The other woman stretched out on the bed on her side, propping up on one elbow. "Let me tell you a story, Beth. It might help."

"I'm not sure I understand."

"Jed and I were high school sweethearts."

"I had no idea."

"Well, it was a long time ago. Up until this summer when he came home for our reunion, I hadn't seen him in a decade."

"That must have been odd."

"Odd and awkward. Because I was the one who broke up with him."

"Ouch."

"Yeah. We were madly in love. He was headed off to college, but he wanted to give me a ring before he left."

"And what about you?"

"I didn't have the money to go to college. My parents and younger brother were killed in a car accident when I was fifteen. There was only a tiny life insurance policy. My grandmother lived with us and was in poor health. So, all during high school I was her caretaker. It was everything I could do to keep my grades up, go out with Jed occasionally and make sure Grammy was looked after."

"That must have been terrible."

"Not terrible, exactly. Just a lot of hard work. But by the time graduation rolled around, I realized that Grammy was sliding into dementia. Jed was brilliant. He had multiple acceptance letters from colleges and universities all over the country. But he chose to go to Austin so he would be able to come home and see me regularly."

"So why did you break it off?"

"I knew it was an impossible situation. He deserved to do all the things young men are supposed to do when they get out on their own. I couldn't bear the thought of dragging him down."

"I see."

"I don't think you do. I made assumptions about his feelings for me. I told myself it was puppy love. That he would meet lots of girls in college—suitable females with family backgrounds similar to his. I did the noble thing and let him go."

"And?"

"I broke his heart," Kimberly said flatly, her eyes shadowed with remembered grief. "And I broke my own. All because I had issues with self-esteem and a chip on my shoulder about my circumstances."

"Why are you telling me all this?"

Kimberly's smile was gentle. "Royal is a small town when all is said and done. I know there have been unkind people over the years who have slandered your reputation. And I remember your mother. She wasn't much of a parent."

"Don't forget my wonderful brother," Beth quipped. Hearing Kimberly voice the truth hurt. A lot.

Kimberly shook her head. "No one who takes the time to know you will ever believe that you are anything but a strong, talented, amazing woman."

Beth refused to cry, though her eyes burned. "Thanks for the pep talk."

"I'm serious, Beth. If there's something between you and Drew…something real, don't be as stupid as I was. Don't throw away love."

"Who said anything about love?"

"I saw the way he looked at you this morning."

"That was lust. There's a difference."

"And which is it for you?"

The pointed question put a lump in Beth's throat and made her stomach hurt. "The man is a billionaire."

"The man is a *man*. We all need someone to love. I've been lucky enough to get a second chance. I don't care how much money Jed has. He loves me, and I love him, and we're having a baby. That's something money can't buy."

Beth jumped to her feet, stripping off the dress and putting on a clean pair of jeans and a long-sleeved lavender top. "Thank you for bringing the clothes. If you'll give me the receipt, I'll write you a check."

Kimberly nodded. "I'll get it to you tomorrow. And listen, Beth, take things slow if you're scared, but don't run away. You and Drew could easily have been killed, but you weren't. Haven't you wondered why?"

"Mother Nature is random in her violence."

"True. But those of us who survived owe a debt to the ones the storm took. We have to live. And be happy. Don't you see?"

Beth understood what Kimberly was saying. And she agreed with it up to a point. Life was precious. To have survived a killer storm was no small thing. But she wasn't sure she trusted her feelings. Or Drew's. Not yet.

Sexual attraction was fickle. It could burn out rapidly.

She glanced at the small pile of clothes on the bed. Kimberly had included everything Beth would need for a quick trip to Dallas and a romantic evening. Jed's fiancée had exquisite taste. Beth would not feel out of place appearing in public with Drew Farrell, the polished and sophisticated businessman.

But donning a costume of sorts only transformed the

outside. Did Drew want to know the real Beth? Or maybe the bigger question was—was Beth willing to trust Drew with her heart and her emotional baggage?

"Thank you, Kimberly," she said. "I don't know how you did it, but everything you brought is perfect."

"I've had a lot of experience." Kimberly smiled. "But that doesn't include maternity clothes. I'm getting close to needing them. My pants are already tight."

"I'm sure your hunky groom-to-be would help you shop."

"I know he would. But there's so much to do after the storm. And we want to get married as soon as possible. I have my eye on a wedding dress downtown with a high waist. Hopefully, the style will disguise the fact that I'm *increasing,* as the old women used to say."

"Drew and I will only be in Dallas overnight. As soon as I get back, I'll pitch in and help you any way I can."

Kimberly hugged her. "I wonder if we'll end up being sisters-in-law?" she said archly.

For a moment, Beth allowed herself to dream. Kimberly was a sweetheart, and Beth had never had a sister. "Let's take care of one romance at a time. You and Jed deserve your special day. Don't worry about Drew and me."

Drew fidgeted in his chair wondering how one simple dinner could last for ten hours. That's how long it seemed. Everyone at the table was in a jolly mood, everyone except him. Jed beamed, happier than Drew had ever seen him. Kimberly glowed visibly, wrapped in the love of her fiancé and the knowledge that a baby was on the way. Even Beth, who often guarded her feelings, laughed and joked and enjoyed the impromptu dinner party.

All Drew cared about was getting Beth naked. The sooner, the better.

The housekeeper had made a pumpkin spice cake for dessert before she went home for the day. The women dished it up, added ice cream, and made coffee while the brothers conferred over what Drew would say in Jed's place tomorrow. When that was nailed down, they stood to help carry bowls and cups to the table.

Drew sat down beside Beth and frowned. "Not to dampen the mood, but I heard some news today about the mystery woman who came to Beth's stand right before the storm."

"Don't keep us in suspense," Jed said.

Beth jumped in. "What about her? Is she worse?"

"No, but they've identified her as Skye Taylor. Her parents still live in Royal and were shocked when the authorities contacted them. She left town four years ago—ran away with Jacob Holt. It was a big scandal. The two families have been feuding for decades. But no one knew Skye was back, and no one has a clue why Jacob isn't with her. Everybody's assuming the baby is Jacob's but no one knows for sure."

"How sad," Kimberly said. "To miss the birth and the bonding time."

For a moment they were all silent. Skye had missed those moments as well, since she'd been in a coma.

Drew grimaced. "Sorry. I shouldn't have brought it up. We're celebrating."

Kimberly patted his hand. "We can't avoid sobering news these days. But life goes on." She gazed askance at the large scoop of vanilla bean in front of her, clearly trying to change the subject. "Is it bad that I'm already having cravings? I could eat this whole bowl and then some."

Jed grinned. "More of you to love."

Drew rolled his eyes. "Does that line really work with women?"

"If it's sincere." Kimberly shook her spoon at him and took another bite. "Am I right, Beth?"

Beth swallowed, dabbed her mouth with a napkin, and frowned slightly. "Yes. I suppose. But I'm more interested in finding a guy who waits on me hand and foot and cooks all my meals and cleans the house."

Laughter greeted her comeback. Drew paused to think about what she had said. The Farrells employed almost a hundred workers at Willowbrook—counting the stable staff, financial managers and the housekeeping crew. In his entire life, Drew had never cooked anything more complicated than a scrambled egg on a propane stove.

His dad had made sure the two Farrell boys could take care of themselves in the wilderness. But on a daily basis, Drew had the luxury of concentrating on business, free from worry about meals or dust bunnies or muddy footprints on the hardwood floors. His life had been, and still was, so very different from Beth's. What she had accomplished all on her own was little short of a miracle.

She would make some man a very good wife.

He sat back in his chair, dessert uneaten, and tried not to let on that he'd just had an epiphany of gigantic proportions. Maybe it was seeing Jed in love. Or perhaps it was the literal earth-moving force of the tornado that had knocked some sense into him. But whatever the impetus, suddenly, he saw his life more clearly.

Willowbrook was a family enterprise. The ranch was far more than a business, it was his heritage, a place made for children. He wasn't getting any younger. He'd spent the last year and a half squabbling with Beth, but maybe underneath it all, he'd been falling for her.

He watched her interact with Kimberly and Jed. She was funny and witty and smart. Jed already treated her like a sister. Drew had acknowledged long ago the physical pull between Beth and him. But now he paused to consider everything he liked about her. Love? Yes. It was possible. All he needed was time to think it over.

Jed insisted on clearing the table. Drew jumped up to help. The women immediately began poring over the notebook and magazines Kimberly pulled from a large tote bag.

Kimberly shook her head when Beth pointed to a picture. "We want to keep this very simple."

The men rejoined them. Jed took Kimberly's hand and squeezed it. "I've done some thinking, sweetheart. If we try to invite a handful of close friends, we're going to end up leaving out people who would love to be here. I grew up in Royal. Drew has lived here all his life. You have, too. I say we call it an informal ceremony and reception and open it up to anyone who wants to come. People could use a breather from the work and the sadness and the stress. It doesn't have to be complicated."

Kimberly paled. "But the businesses in town were hit hard. I don't know that we could find a caterer."

Drew spoke up. "Jed and I have a buddy in Austin who does this kind of thing all the time. He has the chairs and the tents and the food ideas. If you'll trust him, he'll handle it all. You won't need to do a thing except show up."

Kimberly turned to Beth. "What do *you* think?"

Beth nibbled her bottom lip. "Well...."

"Tell me the truth," Kimberly insisted.

"You want to get married right away because of the baby, correct?"

"Yes."

"And we all agree that Royal could use an excuse to concentrate on something other than relief work and insurance claims."

"True."

"Then I say if your future husband and brother-in-law are willing to feed the entire town, let them do it."

Kimberly shook her head, her expression dazed. "I'm not sure I'm ready to be a Farrell."

Jed kissed her cheek. "No choice now. You're mine, honey. I sure as hell am not going to lose you again."

Eleven

Drew closed the front door behind his brother with an inner sigh of relief. Jed was staying at Kimberly's again tonight. Which left Drew alone with Beth, just the way he liked it. He found her in the kitchen tidying up. "Leave that," he said.

"It won't take a minute." She continued putting things away.

Leaning in the doorway, Drew watched her. Tall and leggy, she was beautiful enough to be a model. But there was something so real about her. She was a poster child for the girl next door. Which in Drew's case was literally true.

He moved behind her, slipping his arms around her waist and linking his hands over her belly. "I want to make love to you tonight."

Beth turned suddenly, startling him. Wary eyes looked into his. She scanned his face as though looking for some kind of answer to a question he didn't understand. "I want that, too. But I haven't been entirely honest with you. I'd like to clear the air before we go any further."

His arousal plummeted. Releasing her, he grabbed a kitchen chair, turned it backward and straddled the seat, resting his arms on the back. "I'm listening." He couldn't imagine what she was going to say, and it rattled him.

She remained by the sink, arms wrapped around her

waist, her body language defensive. "It's no secret that I came from the wrong side of the tracks. My dad left when I was three. My mom was an alcoholic who made it from day to day with odd jobs and public assistance. People around Royal knew her, because she wasn't above begging on street corners. She wasn't intentionally abusive to my brother and me, but let's just say that by the time I was a teenager, I knew I wanted more for my life."

"Where is she now?"

"She died of pneumonia when I was a senior in high school. Her health was in such bad shape that she couldn't fight it off."

"I'm sorry, Beth."

"It's a scary world when the only parent you've ever known, even a bad one, leaves you. But I was lucky to have good teachers who helped me get a scholarship to the University of Texas at Austin."

He kept his expression impassive, though his response was gut deep. "So far this doesn't sound like a tale of defeat."

"Be patient. I'm getting there. While I was in school, I did work-study and also two other part-time gigs, one waitressing and the other tutoring kids in math."

"Math?"

"Don't sound so surprised. That was my major. I minored in marketing."

"I'm impressed. No wonder everyone knows about your produce stand."

"Well, anyway," she said, "by the time I graduated, I was missing Royal. Not my family in particular. As I told you before, we're not close. But I grew up in Royal, all eighteen years before I went off to school. As wonderful as Austin was, it wasn't home. I guess I had deeper roots here than I realized."

"So you came home."

"Not yet. You're getting ahead of me." She continued her story, her quiet voice drawing him in. "I met a man."

Drew stiffened, hoping she didn't notice. For some inexplicable reason, he wasn't sure he wanted to hear this part. He liked the notion of Beth Andrews as sweet and untouched. What did that say about him? She was twenty-eight years old. A truly extraordinary woman in every way, particularly when it came to her stunning looks. It didn't make sense to think that no man had ever staked a claim.

He prompted her. "Tell me about him."

The long silence grew heavy. "He was older."

"How much older?"

"Eighteen years. We patronized the same video store, back when there were such things. One day he chatted me up and invited me out for coffee."

"So he was forty?"

"Almost. But his wife had died of leukemia when they were both little more than newlyweds. He never remarried."

"And then you entered the picture." He was really trying not to be critical, but this unknown bum sounded like a guy hitting on a college girl while in the midst of a midlife crisis. It made no difference that Beth had been of legal age.

She picked up on his ambivalence. "It's not what you think. We genuinely cared about each other. I've always been mature for my age, and he was lonely."

"I'll bet."

The sarcastic retort silenced her.

Drew grimaced. "I'm sorry. I was being a jerk. Tell me the rest. What was his name?"

"Richard," she said. "His name was Richard."

"Finish your story, please."

"Are you sure you want to hear it?"

"I really do."

She wished the recounting put her in a better light. At the time it hadn't seemed so bad. But in retrospect, the decisions she had made were ones she mostly regretted.

"We became close," she said.

"Physically intimate?"

"Yes."

"Was he your first lover?"

"No. I'd had one boyfriend in college. Nothing too serious. My lack of experience was really ironic, because somehow in high school I gained a reputation for being easy."

"I don't understand."

"Guys wanted to go out with me because I had nice breasts and blond hair. I also came from a part of town and from a family that gave people certain impressions of me. When boys realized that I didn't put out on a date, they were embarrassed, because they thought I had been fooling around with their buddies. So to save face, they made up stories. Denying them only drew attention to me, so I kept my mouth shut."

She had no clue what Drew was thinking. Some people assumed that all scandalous gossip had basis in fact.

His gaze was steady. "I'm sorry, Beth. That must have been excruciating."

The sincere caring in his voice brought tears to her eyes, but she blinked them away rapidly. She had long since come to terms with her past. That was one reason her little house and farm were so special. There, she was her own person.

"Well, anyway…back to Richard. He was a lovely man, decent and kind. Though he definitely wasn't a father figure, he was a mentor, I suppose. While I was with him, he taught me about life in many ways. Simple things such as how to choose a wine, but deeper stuff, too, like not settling for a man who treated me poorly."

"Where is he now? Why did you break up?"

"We didn't break up. He knew I wanted to come home to Royal. But I still had a few student loans. Without a car and cash to make the move, I was stuck."

"Did he ask you to stay with him?"

"He wanted to, I think. But he was the sort of man who put others' needs ahead of his own. He told me that the road was wide open in front of me…that I would have experiences and opportunities to find my passion in life. He knew before I did that I *loved* him, but I wasn't *in love* with him. And I respected him too much to pretend."

"So what happened?"

Here was the part she wanted to skip. But Drew had heard everything else. "He opened a checking account for me and deposited twenty-five thousand dollars. Then he bought me a car, gave me his blessing and sent me on my way."

She saw and heard Drew inhale sharply. What was he thinking? She wanted badly to know. In all fairness, what she had done *could be* construed as sex for money. It wasn't. Not at all. She knew that. But the facts were open to interpretation.

"What did you do with the cash?"

Though she listened carefully, she was unable to detect any note of judgment in his question. "I used the least amount possible to make it back here to Royal. Took only what was necessary to put down a deposit on an apartment. I'd been home five days when I landed a job working at one of the banks downtown as a teller. It wasn't what I wanted, but it paid the bills."

"And the rest of Richard's gift?"

"It stayed in my account for several years until I used it as a down payment to buy the farm."

Drew sat in silence absorbing the details of Beth's remarkable story. Though he still wasn't happy with the unknown Richard, the man deserved kudos for doing what was best for Beth.

The one thing Drew hadn't questioned was the status of the relationship today. Were Beth and Richard still friends? Did they call and text and visit occasionally? Beth was twenty-eight, which meant that the mysterious Richard had to be about forty-six. Still plenty young enough to remarry and start a family, especially with a younger wife.

It was entirely possible that in the intervening years Beth's feelings toward her benefactor might have changed…deepened. On the other hand, the way she kissed Drew didn't suggest an attachment to another man.

He stood up. What she shared with him suggested a level of trust. He was humbled by her openness, especially since his treatment of her in the past had been questionable at best.

Beth watched him walk toward her. "So, do you still want me…knowing the truth? I might be a gold-digger luring you into my bed so I can get my hands on your money."

"For the record, that has never crossed my mind." He grinned. "And to be perfectly clear, you can put your hands on anything I've got." He tilted her mouth to meet his. Her lips were soft and eager, her body pliant in his embrace. The scent of cinnamon and spices lingered in the air. Drew's arousal built from gentle enjoyment to flat-out desperation at warp speed.

He scooped her into his arms and strode down the corridor toward his bedroom. "As for whether I still want you? I think you know the answer to that."

Beth laughed softly. With one hand she traced the shell of his ear. The fact that an innocent touch could inflict so much damage to his self-control told him things were different. *Beth* was different. The ball was in his court, though. He was determined to show her how much they had to give each other.

He kicked open the bedroom door so hard it bounced off the wall. Never pausing, he strode to the bed and went down with her, tumbling in a melee of arms and legs.

"We have our shoes on," Beth protested. "You'll ruin the spread."

"Screw the spread," he groaned. But to pacify her, he toed off his cowboy boots and waited impatiently until she managed to get rid of her ballet flats.

She sat cross-legged and stared at him. "Don't move. I want to unbutton your shirt."

Breathing harshly, he leaned back on his elbows and waited. She knelt beside him with an endearingly serious look on her face. Slender fingers worked the buttons free of their buttonholes. Everywhere her fingers brushed his skin, he burned.

When she was done, she sat back on her heels. "You are a very handsome man," she said quietly.

Her solemn praise made him uncomfortable. He worked outside much of his life, sometimes shirtless, and never thought twice about it. His naturally golden skin was permanently tanned. But having the woman he wanted study him so closely threatened his equilibrium.

He scooted back against the pillows and feigned relaxation with his hands tucked behind his head. "Your turn. Take off your shirt. And go slowly. I plan to enjoy this."

Though she didn't respond verbally, Beth met his challenge with an innocent strip tease that dried his mouth. When she slid her arms out of the top and tossed it aside, all that was left was a sheer bra whose delicate fabric did nothing to conceal her rose-colored nipples.

"Come here," he groaned, extending his arms. "I can't wait anymore."

She went to him willingly, settling half across his chest, kissing him teasingly. "I think we're overdressed," she muttered, her hips pressed to his.

He was hard and ready. His chest heaved with harsh pants. "We have a fifteen minute pants-on rule in this bed. Otherwise, I'll embarrass myself."

They kissed for hours it seemed. Exploratory. Urgent. Passionate. Tender. Every flavor and permutation of lip-to-lip known to man. Like teenagers necking in the backseat of a car.

Beth must have lost some weight in the aftermath of the tragedy. He was able to slide his palm down inside her jeans and underwear, finding the firm swells of her butt and caressing them. She buried her face against his neck, biting his collarbone.

He flinched. Desire roared in his head, blinding him to everything but the need to possess her. "I want you naked," he muttered.

"I thought you'd never ask." She scooted away from him and removed the rest of her clothes.

He raced her instinctively. When they were both bare as the day they were born, they met in the center of the bed—kneeling—breathless....

"I can't believe it's taken me this long to realize what I was missing." He rubbed a thumb across her flushed cheek. "I want you so much it's insane."

"Insane bad? Or insane good?" The sparkle in her eyes made him uncomfortable. Beth Andrews knew exactly what she did to him. Of course, in this particular scenario, it was difficult to hide.

He cupped her neck with two hands. "You're important to me, Beth. This isn't casual sex."

He said it to reassure her. Instead, she bit her lip, a sure sign of her agitation. "Don't say things you'll regret later, Drew. Our whole world is topsy-turvy right now. But that's no reason to make a grand gesture. I'm here because I want to be. For now. Let's leave it at that."

Several arguments sprang to mind, but when both her hands closed around his erection, he found it was impossible to string words together. His body tightened in helpless pleasure. When she flinched, he realized he had gripped her shoulders too tightly. "Sorry."

"I like it," she said, grinning. "I like knowing I drive you crazy."

If the situation hadn't been so loaded with physical and emotional baggage, Beth might have laughed out loud. Apparently she had shocked him.

She wanted to say, *I like knowing you're mine.* But that might have been over the line.

Even so, she let the concept roll around in her head while they eased by unspoken consent down onto the mattress. Drew paused only long enough to take care of protection. When she was flat on her back with him looming over her on one elbow, she took a deep breath and exhaled slowly, trying to steady her nerves. No one had ever made her feel this way. No one.

She wanted to crawl inside his skin until there was no more him and her, but only them. After a lifetime of guarding her emotions and holding back in every relationship, sexual or otherwise, she wanted to open herself to Drew. "I don't want to scare you," she said softly, "but I think you're pretty wonderful."

His grin, a flash of white teeth and cocky confidence,

revealed his playful side. "A compliment from my arch rival?" He kissed her nose. "I thought we survived the tornado, but maybe the world is coming to an end."

"Smart ass." She lifted her hips, hoping he would get the idea. "I argued with you on numerous occasions, but that didn't stop me from ogling your butt and wondering what you would be like in bed."

He shifted, rubbing his sex in the notch of her thighs. "Why, Ms. Andrews. How naughty of you."

Dizziness, the wonderful kind, made her eyes close for a moment. Her senses intensified. Inhaling the spicy aroma of his aftershave…feeling the warmth of his breath on her skin. Every second took on new meaning. The hoarseness in his voice told her that he felt the same alluring possibilities.

"Go slow," she pleaded. "I don't want it to end."

A low, raw curse underscored his ferocity as he entered her in one forceful thrust that shook the bed.

She was so primed she nearly came. Her breathing shallow, she managed a weak question. "You call that slow?"

He rested his forehead on hers. "Sorry. I'll do better."

"Any better, and you'll kill us both."

A laugh rumbled through his chest. "Is it really possible to die from too much pleasure? My life insurance is up to date, but I'm sure Jed's expecting us to be at the wedding."

The wedding. For one weak, poignant second, Beth allowed herself to imagine a *double* wedding. What would it be like to know that a man like Drew loved her unconditionally? Enough to put a ring on her finger….

Pushing away the inopportune fantasy, she concentrated on the delicious present. "I know CPR," she whispered, nipping his bottom lip with her teeth. "If we climb too high, I'll take care of you."

The notion that Drew needed *anyone's* care, much less

hers, was almost comical. He had everything as far as she could tell. Maybe not a wife with a baby on the way. But home and hearth weren't a lure for every bachelor. Drew jetted all over the world. He probably had women available on every continent. She believed he cared about her. She really did. If nothing else, the tornado had proved what kind of man he was. He had literally saved her life.

"You *do* make me crazy," he muttered.

It didn't sound like a compliment. She squeezed him intimately where her body clasped his. How long could he hold out? She had asked for slow, but already she regretted that request. Inside her he was thick and ready, pulsing with an energy that promised to consume her. "I changed my mind," she panted. "I don't want to wait."

"Patience is a virtue."

Since he said it through clenched teeth, she didn't put too much stock in the platitude. "Virtue is overrated. Take me, Drew. Hard. Please."

Her about-face snapped whatever chains held him in place. "Whatever the lady wants." Withdrawing slowly, he thrust again, setting up a rhythm designed to drive them both mad. She clung to his shoulders, her legs wrapped around his waist. Reveling in his wildness, she took everything he had to give and responded in kind.

She grabbed his hair and pulled. "More," she cried. "More."

He hit a pleasure point one last time and she came apart, flying into the dark without a net. Dimly, she heard him shout his own release.

It was too much and not enough. But in the end, all she could do was cling to him and live in the moment.

Drew slept, but he kept a tight hold on Beth. Even his subconscious knew that she was a flight risk. She felt right in his bed. As though they had been together forever. He needed time to think, to plan.

Toward morning he made love to her one last time. Slow and sweet, their coupling built on soft touches, quiet gasps, shuddered completion. It was all he could do to force himself to let her go.

"I never want to leave this bed," he said, smoothing a hand down her back. "But the chopper is going to be here in an hour." He kissed her shoulder. "I'll have one of the staff put a suitcase outside your door in the next half hour. Can you get ready that quickly? Throw your things in the bag. We'll have someone at the hotel press whatever you need." The fact that she grumbled and lingered despite the timetable was gratifying.

"Lucky for you I'm low maintenance," she said. She nuzzled her face in the side of his neck, her breasts pressed against his chest. "I'm going, I'm going."

He was treated to a brief but memorable naked tableau as Beth grabbed up her things and dressed rapidly. She shot him a glance over her shoulder as she dashed for the door. "Shouldn't you be moving?"

"Didn't want to miss the floor show." He was still laughing when she disappeared.

Drew shouldn't have been surprised when his houseguest was true to her word. Beth met him in the foyer at five minutes before her allotted deadline. He almost did a double take. He was so accustomed to seeing her in casual clothes that he was stunned to see an entirely different woman.

Her long hair was twisted up in one of those fancy styles on the back of her head. Kimberly's fashion choices had been spot on. The pencil skirt and short jacket in navy pinstripe showcased Beth's narrow waist and curvy bosom.

And her legs. Wow. Pin-up girls would kill to have those gams. Taupe pumps with four-inch heels drew attention to shapely calves and trim ankles.

He whistled long and low, eyeing her from head to toe. "For a farmer, you clean up real nice."

Beth turned in a slow circle, smiling. "We have Kimberly to thank for that. She turned a pumpkin into a fancy pie."

"You're too modest. And if that was a Cinderella reference, I'll have to buy you a book of fairytales when we get to Dallas. Anyone who botches a classic that badly needs a refresher course."

Her smile faded. "I know the story, Drew. Every little girl does. But we aren't exactly going to a ball, now are we?"

The front door swung open without warning, and two of the ranch hands came in to collect the bags. "Your ride is here, Mr. Farrell. Whenever you're ready," said one of the men respectfully.

Drew took Beth's arm as they made their way to the concrete pad. The grassy expanse between the house and their destination was uneven and not easily traversed in couture footwear.

The pilot had shut off the rotors, so there was no wind to contend with. But the high step presented some problems for Beth. Drew didn't wait for the inevitable argument. He lifted her by the waist and set her inside the doorway of the chopper.

She looked down at him and shook her head. "I'm not a package. You could have asked first."

"I know you. We'd have spent fifteen minutes dithering while you tried to figure out how to climb aboard in that skirt. I merely speeded up the process." He climbed in as well, greeted the pilot, and handed Beth a set of head-phones. "Fasten your seat belt, honey. And hang on."

Beth left her stomach somewhere down at the ranch along with her determination to appear poised and confident. She felt like a kid on a ride at the amusement part, half thrilled, half scared spitless. The ground fell away so fast her knuckles turned white as she held on to the edge of her seat.

Drew leaned into her and shouted. "What do you think?"

Gazing at the vista below, she shook her head in amazement. "I love it."

She wasn't sure if he heard her or not, but they exchanged a smile that made her stomach flip. It would have been nice to blame the woozy feeling on the combination of speed and altitude. But in truth, when Drew took her hand in his and gripped it tightly, she experienced a flash of perfect joy...one of those brief moments that linger in the heart always.

For a girl from the wrong side of the tracks who had never been more than ten feet off the ground, it was heady stuff.

The trip was over far too quickly. They landed atop one of Dallas's tallest buildings on a helipad marked with red and black paint. The pilot set them perfectly within the lines. When the rotors stilled at last, the lack of noise was jarring.

Drew tapped her chin. "Close your mouth, country mouse. You'll catch flies."

His gentle teasing made her blush. "I can't believe this is commonplace to you. I feel like a movie star."

He jumped down onto the pad and reached up to help her out. "You look like one, too. C'mon. I've got twenty minutes to spare. I'll get someone to call a cab and take you on to the hotel with our luggage."

"Can't I stay with you during the meeting? Or would that be a faux pas?"

"But wouldn't you rather relax?"

"I want to see you in action," she said. "Especially if you're stepping in for Jed. I've been on the receiving end of your Big-Bad-Wolf routine, remember?"

Drew scowled. "Jed is no pussycat, despite his present lovesick condition. I'm more or less a silent partner. He's the shrewd businessman."

She patted his arm as they stepped into the building via an industrial gray metal door. After the bright sunshine, she was momentarily blinded. "Does that mean you see love as a weakness?"

He paused in the shadows to kiss her quickly. "Don't put words in my mouth."

His lips were firm and warm. She inhaled the scent of starched cotton and expensive cologne. Seeing him in a suit and tie this morning had weakened her resolve not to weave daydreams. The cowboy businessman managed to look both professional and sexy at the same time. His arm was hard against her back, dragging her so close they touched in all sorts of interesting places.

"I stand corrected," she said, when he allowed her to breathe.

Now that her eyes had adjusted to the dim lighting at the top of the staircase, she could see that his gaze was unusually dark and fathomless.

"I admire my younger brother more than any other man I know. And I am happy for him, honest to God happy for him. You and I should be so lucky."

All the breath left her lungs. Though it took courage, she felt recklessly brave. "What does that mean?"

He kissed her again, before glancing at his watch with an imprecation. "I think you can figure it out, Beth. But it will have to keep."

Life had taught Beth some tough lessons about expectations and their demise. But hearing Drew's cryptic answer filled her with a quiet, warm jubilance. She felt no need to press. It was enough to hoard the amazing surprise and wait for things to develop. Drew was not the kind of man to make promises he didn't intend to keep.

Besides, the next few days were all about Jed and Kimberly. No one should steal their thunder, least of all Beth and Drew. If there were things to be said, Drew was right. It could keep. After all, anticipation was the best part of the journey.

It was eye-opening to watch him in action. The sleek boardroom in the sophisticated high rise where Jed had his offices was a pleasing blend of modern with old Texas. The enormous windows offered breathtaking views of the Dallas skyline. Though the furniture was unmistakably twenty-first century, the dark wood and a definite streak of tradition still made a statement.

Drew settled into the chair at the head of the table. Beth quietly took a seat along the wall with a dozen young men and women who were apparently staffers or interns. Jed, a financial genius according to Drew, managed funds for a large consortium of Texas ranchers. This quarterly meeting was routine but important.

After a brief apology for Jed's unavoidable absence—without going into inappropriate personal detail—Drew launched into the agenda. Beth watched him carefully, seeing him as others did. He wielded an air of command and confidence that was not only a product of his privileged upbringing but integral to who he was as a man.

The wealthy and influential ranchers seated around the

table, Jed's board of directors, afforded Drew respect and careful attention. What she hadn't expected was the wit and humor Drew infused into dry numbers and projections. His relaxed style produced laughter, camaraderie and a speedy conclusion to what could have been an endless discussion.

He didn't draw any kind of attention to Beth, and she was glad. Being a fly on the wall was all she wanted. By the time Drew adjourned the meeting and spoke to numerous individuals afterward, her stomach was growling. They had been up early, and it was almost one o'clock.

At last, as the room emptied, he joined her. "Well, how did I do?"

She linked her arm through his. "You were a lot nicer to this group than you ever were to me. But maybe that's because none of them own land you want to steal."

Pressing his hand over her mouth, he shook his head in mock disgust. "Why are you the only person who thinks of me as a villain?"

She twisted free, gazing at him almost eye-to-eye thanks to her borrowed footwear. "If the twirly mustache fits...."

With a chuckle, he ushered her in front of him. "Let's get out of here. I'm off the clock, and I promised you some fun."

Drew wanted to skip lunch and anything else in his way and take her straight to the hotel. Beth deserved more than that, though. She'd shown him bits and pieces of her difficult childhood, but the parts she left out were pretty clear when he read between the lines. Except for college—where she had lived on a shoestring budget—Beth had led a narrowly confined life. No travel. No cultural opportunities.

He felt a moment of shame for taking so much of his

life for granted. Despite his physical hunger, he wanted to please Beth...to make her happy. And that's what he set out to do.

After an intimate lunch, they started with one of the art museums. Two hours later when Beth expressed an interest in Dallas's sobering Kennedy history, they headed for Dealey Plaza.

Drew couldn't remember the last time he had played tourist. He'd forgotten how much fun it could be. As the day progressed, the truth cemented itself firmly in his gut. He no longer wanted to fight with his neighbor. He wanted to make peace, even at the expense of his own endeavors.

They went back to the hotel only long enough to shower and change for dinner. Beth refused to give him a peek at her dress. As he waited impatiently in the suite's opulent sitting room, she finally came through the door.

"Wow." It was the only word he could muster. The black dress she wore revealed lots of skin. Beautiful, creamy skin....

The quiet pleasure in her eyes warmed him. He kissed her cheek, unwilling to do more for fear they wouldn't make it out the door. "I've never enjoyed a business trip as much as I did today," he said, trying to make light of the emotions bombarding him. His heart pounded.

Beth smoothed her skirt with both hands and wrinkled her nose, betraying a hint of nerves. "I've had fun, too."

"C'mon," he said gruffly. "I promised you dinner and dancing. Your chariot awaits."

Twelve

Beth was living a fairytale. She knew it. And acknowledged it wouldn't last. But she decided to enjoy herself and appreciate the moment.

When Drew helped her step into the sleek black limo parked at the curb of their upscale hotel, she felt like a princess. As they glided through the heavy Dallas traffic, he served her a glass of champagne. "To the future," he said, clinking his glass gently against hers.

She took a sip of the sparkling liquid, relishing the crisp bite and feeling the bubbles tickle her nose. "To the future."

Their toast covered a host of possibilities. Though the storm had decimated much of Royal, the town would rebuild and emerge stronger than before. Jed and Kimberly were getting married. Soon, Drew would have a niece or nephew. But did his quiet words hold a deeper meaning?

They sat on opposite ends of the wide seat. Drew seemed distracted, his attention focused now on the passing view.

She finished her drink and twirled the stem of the glass in her fingers, wishing she had the guts to slide across the space separating her from Drew and put a hand on his thigh. The open window behind the driver stifled the impulse. Not only that, but Drew's dark suit made him seem less approachable than the man she knew as a down-to-earth cowboy. A very wealthy cowboy, but a man of the land, nevertheless.

This Drew she had met in Dallas was more sophisticated, perhaps even a bit more dangerous. She would give a lot to know what he was thinking.

Their destination was a private club. Inside, the lighting was romantic and the décor stunning. A supercilious maître d' led them to a table for two tucked away in an intimate corner.

Beth barely tasted her fork-tender beef, though it was some of Texas's finest. Drew talked. And she talked. They flirted. They laughed. Books. Movies. Politics. Nothing about her family or his. Nothing about the storm.

When the last bites of cherry tart were nothing but crumbs, Drew held out his hand. "I've been waiting all night for this."

The polished hardwood dance floor in the center of the room was covered in shards of light from the priceless chandelier overhead. Couples of all ages moved in time to the vintage band that played classic romantic tunes. The common denominator in the room was wealth and tradition.

When Drew took her in his arms, he settled one big, warm palm on her back. She leaned into him, resting her cheek on his broad shoulder. She'd never had much occasion to dance formally, but his confidence steered them smoothly.

Letting the music wash over her, she floated—mentally and physically—her thoughts flitting as comfortably as her feet followed his. Publicly acceptable foreplay. That's what it was. He held her so close she felt the heat of his body. Their heartbeats seemed in sync.

It was impossible to miss his arousal. Hers was easier to

hide but no less urgent. Her muscles were lax with sensory overload. Every cell in her body trembled with anticipation.

When he spoke, his warm breath teased her ear. "I could hold you like this all night. But whenever you want to leave, say the word."

"One more song," she pleaded. "One more dance…."

It must have been late. She had lost all track of time. If it weren't for the promise of what lay ahead, she might have chosen to dance until the club closed down. Drew's fingers stroked her bare back above the edge of her dress. The gentle caress was at once soothing and sensual.

The band took a break, waving at the crowd and exiting the stage. Beth pulled away and smiled. "I think that's our cue."

On the ride back to the hotel, she and Drew did not sit apart. He tucked his arm around her and pulled her close.

"More champagne?" he asked.

"No, thank you." She wanted to remember every second of the night ahead. Alcohol would only make her sleepy.

Somehow they made it from the limo to the elevator to their suite. But the details were fuzzy. In the sitting room, Drew ripped off his tie and discarded his jacket, tossing both on a chair. Beth stepped out of her shoes and wiggled her toes in relief. The plush carpet felt wonderful. For a woman used to tromping around farm fields, an entire evening in high heels was torture.

She and Drew stood half a room apart. When he crooked his finger with a wicked smile, her stomach did a free-fall. Fingering one of the rhinestone straps of her dress, she lifted her chin, determined to be his match, at least in the bedroom. "You seem to think I'll coming running whenever you ask."

Two masculine eyebrows went up. "I'm perfectly willing to reverse the roles if the lady wishes."

Damn him. She smothered a grin. It was impossible to win a battle of wits with Drew. At least when it came to sex. She decided to call his bluff. Slowly, watching his eyes darken and glaze with hunger, she slipped the narrow jeweled straps off her shoulders. The dress didn't fall. It fit snugly around her breasts.

With one hand she lifted her skirt and carefully peeled off a pair of naughty undies, stepping out of them with flair.

Drew's Adam's apple bobbed conspicuously. She was pretty sure she saw a sheen of sweat on his forehead.

Tossing the scrap of black silk in his direction, she sauntered into the bedroom.

Drew shuddered, blinking his eyes to clear his vision. He forced himself to count to ten…and then to fifty. His blood pressure went up, not down. Unbuttoning his cuffs as he walked, he made his way slowly to the room where Beth waited for him. The lack of speed was intentional. He had to gather himself, needed to clear his head.

When he paused in the open doorway, all his plans were for naught. Beth stood naked beside the bed with her back to him. She whirled around, the dress clutched to her chest. "Hello."

Perfect white teeth dug a furrow in her bottom lip. Her slender body, what he could see of it, was healthy and shapely. For one long moment, he literally couldn't speak. She dazzled him. Finally, he cleared his throat. "Hello."

Their stilted conversation might have been humorous if the mood in the room hadn't been heavy with sexual tension.

She sat on the edge of the bed, still covering her interesting bits with the dress. "Is there something you wanted to say to me?"

The overhead light was off, but the bedside lamp glowed. He shrugged. "It occurred to me you might think I invited you along on this trip so I could have wild, crazy sex with you."

"Well, didn't you?"

"Yes. I mean no. Oh hell, Beth. It's way more than that and you know it." He was frustrated…and as awkward as a teenage boy courting his first girl. "You know the saying, 'actions speak louder than words'?"

"Of course."

"That's what I'm going with." The time for talking was over.

While she sat and watched, he undressed…completely. He saw Beth assess his condition. Color flooded her cheeks. He was fully erect. In fact, he'd been hard to one degree or another most of the day. Right now, he felt like a man who hadn't had a woman in years.

He sat down beside her, their hips touching…sans clothing. Beth didn't protest when he tugged the dress out of her grasp and flung it aside. But she had trouble meeting his eyes.

Rubbing her bare knee, he spoke to her softly. "I don't think you can come close to imagining how much I want you at this very moment."

Her quick sideways glance held a hint of hesitation. "You've been with a lot of women."

It could have been an accusation, but it sounded more like a statement of fact. "I'm thirty-two years old," he said quietly. "I've had a number of relationships. But none in the last year."

"Why not?"

"It's been a busy time. We've expanded the ranch operations. I've courted new clients around the world. I suppose

I've become more selective when it comes to sex. Casual hook-ups don't do it for me anymore."

"I still think we're not a good match."

He debated what to say…how to get around the walls she was erecting. "I respect your opinion, Beth, but I reserve the right to prove you wrong."

His gentle teasing finally coaxed a smile from her. "Fair enough."

Without moving away from him, she reached up and began removing the pins from her hair. Thick strands tumbled onto her shoulders. He wrapped one silky blond curl around his fist, waiting until she was finished to pull her close for a kiss. "Come here, Beth."

She slid her arms around his neck, clinging tightly. "Is this where you try to change my mind?"

He laughed roughly. "I'll do my best."

His tongue dueled with hers. Despite her air of toughness, Beth had an innocence about her that made him want to set the moon at her feet, to wrap up the world as a gift and place it in her keeping. She deserved everything he could offer.

Scooping her into his lap, he chuckled when she tried to keep his hands from roaming.

"That tickles," she complained.

He played with one raspberry nipple until it puckered enticingly. "You have the most amazing body." When he switched to the other breast, Beth caught her breath and moaned in a low, throaty gasp that made his skin tighten.

Reading her verbal clues, he eased her down onto the bed and splayed her legs. Her eyes were closed. He was able to take her by surprise. Pinning her thighs with his hands, he bent and tasted her center.

Beth cried out, struggling instinctively.

"Easy, darlin'." He rested his head on her belly and

reached down to stroke her with his fingertips, sliding them back and forth on either side of her most sensitive spot.

Her fingernails scored his forearm. *"Drew!"*

He paused instantly, alarm skittering down his spine. "What's wrong?"

She reared up on her elbows, hair tousled, eyelids at half-mast, lips swollen from his kisses. "How do you know I like that?"

"Was I supposed to ask permission?"

Her expression was one part petulance and two parts reluctant excitement. "I don't think it's a good thing for a man to know so much about women. It gives you an unfair advantage."

"How so?" he asked, genuinely curious.

"What if we have incredible, earth-moving sex, you ruin me for other men, and then we break up?"

He pushed her back onto the bed, chuckling at her imaginary scenario. "I guess that's a risk we'll have to take."

The risk is all mine. She knew it, and she didn't care. Not when Drew made love to her so very well. She closed her eyes a second time and let sensation wash over her. His fingers were both delicate and precise. One moment she hovered on the edge and the next he drew her back, playing with her masterfully.

Hot need coalesced deep in her abdomen. Her body wept for him, moist and ready. As she hovered on the verge of violent release, he thrust two fingers inside her passage and found the spot that triggered her climax.

"Drew. Drew…."

She lost her voice in the middle of the storm. Wrenched with physical pleasure that was incredibly intense, she had no recourse but to let him hold her tightly until everything was calm.

Shaken and bemused, she felt something inside her shift and settle. Drew. It was always going to be Drew for her. That was a damned scary future to contemplate. She felt as fluttery and faint as a Victorian maiden. Of course, most women would be a little woozy after an orgasm like that.

So maybe if he was really serious…maybe she could learn how to be married to a wealthy Texas rancher. Things like entertaining and hobnobbing with the rich and famous. Still, one part of her held back…the little piece of her heart that had survived disappointment after disappointment while she was growing up. Trust was hard. For two years Drew had tried to force her to submit to his wishes concerning their disputes.

Though it was difficult to admit, a tiny suspicion remained. What if he was softening her up so he could persuade her to leave the farm? Even the thought of it made her ill. She had worked hard to make something of her life, despite her upbringing. Surely Drew wouldn't be so cavalier. Surely he respected her feelings.

He scooted her up in the bed. "Your skin is freezing, woman. Let's get under the covers."

She followed his lead, settling into his arms with a sigh of contentment, pushing her doubts aside. The elegant duvet was thick and fluffy. It felt wonderful to cuddle with her sexy, um…*lover? Neighbor? Friend?* What should she call him? Or did it really matter?

Smiling to herself, she roved beneath the covers until her hand encountered hard male flesh. Drew's only reaction was a hissed intake of breath. Lazily, she circled the head of his shaft, feeling the drops of fluid that signaled his excitement. Even without that evidence, his rigid muscles and harsh breathing told her everything.

She stroked him gently, feeling his erection flex and thicken even more. Despite her recent carnal excess, Drew's arousal rekindled a buzz in places she had been sure were sated. Nipping the side of his neck, she moved her hand lower, cupping him intimately. "How do you want me?" she whispered.

He let out a broken laugh. "Six ways to Sunday," he said, humor in his voice despite the tension gripping him. "But I'll settle for good ol' missionary right now. You make me a little nuts, so I'd like to play to my strengths this first time."

Pleased by his wry admission, she shifted onto her back and lifted her arms toward the ceiling. "Take me, I'm yours," she said in her best dramatic voice.

He rolled on a condom and moved on top of her in a nanosecond. "Has anyone ever told you you're a brat?"

"Not recently."

He settled between her thighs, his weight mostly supported on his elbows. "You make me happy, Beth."

She hadn't expected that. Tears sprang to her eyes. His gaze was unguarded, intimate.

"You're not so bad yourself," she said. The flip answer embarrassed her. "Sorry. You took me off guard." Pausing, she searched for the right words. "I admire you, Drew. But more than that, I *like* you. And it doesn't hurt that you're sexy and smart."

"Who knew?" he said with a wry grin.

"Who knew what?"

"That dueling neighbors could end up like this."

She put her hands on his buttocks, feeling his muscular flanks. "But remember, it took a tornado to get us together."

"I suppose that means we're both pretty stubborn."

"True."

"You do something to me I can't explain."

Her heart stopped. She wasn't sure she could respond in kind. Not because it wasn't true, but because the words made her so very vulnerable. Finally, when the silence became too painful, she whispered, "I care about you, too."

He entered her slowly, giving her tenderness and understanding despite her reservations. He was big and dominant and determined.

There was no talking after that. Drew moved in her with barely restrained ferocity. He rolled suddenly, settling her on top of him. "Come with me," he demanded. "Both of us...together." He used his thumb to tease the little bundle of nerves, making her squirm. "I can wait."

"It's too soon."

"Think positive."

Ripples of sensation rolled through her lower abdomen. "Drew...." She swallowed hard.

"Yes, darlin'?"

"You get started. I'll catch up."

He took her at her word. Hard masculine fingers gripped her butt as he urged her up and down. Every stroke took her temperature higher. Drew groaned and shook, nearing the finish.

"Now, baby," he muttered. "Let it go."

The moment took her by surprise, jerking her over the top without warning. Sending her into the abyss. But as she tumbled, she clung to Drew. Sated at the end, they rolled into each other's arms and slept.

Drew frowned in his sleep. Some noise, a damned annoying ping, had dragged him from a deep, wonderful slumber. He opened his eyes, marginally aware that faint light shone in through a crack in the draperies. Beth lay on her side facing away, but curled against him, her bottom bumping his hip.

He touched her hair lightly. Glancing at the digital clock on the bedside table blearily, he managed to make out the numbers. *7:15?* Who in the hell was texting him at this hour of the morning? Yawning, he reached for his phone. Jed's cell number appeared with a message:

Come home as soon as you can. Wedding day after tomorrow. Caterer's only open date. God help us. J J

Jed really must be in love. Drew couldn't remember a single other instance where his brother had used a smiley face, much less two.

Beth sat up, the sheet clutched to her breasts. "Is something wrong?" With her hair tumbled around her face, she looked sexy and adorable.

He handed her his cell phone. Her eyes widened as she read the words. "Day after tomorrow? Seriously? Kimberly must be frantic."

"I knew we had to go home today, but I didn't expect it to be quite so abrupt. Especially since checkout is not until eleven."

"And how did you plan to spend those last three hours?"

He took the phone and dropped it on the carpet. "The same way I'm going to spend the next thirty minutes."

Beth dressed more casually for the return trip. But the navy slacks and pale gold silk blouse were still a far cry from her usual wardrobe. Because Drew had been so inventive in delaying their departure, they barely had a chance to shower and pack their bags. By the time they checked out, grabbed a cab and returned to the office building where the helipad was located, they were several minutes past their agreed upon rendezvous.

The pilot was unfazed, choosing to lean against the building and have a smoke while he waited.

Beth felt as if the morning's sexual antics were emblazoned across her crimson cheeks. Drew merely laughed at her and slid an arm around her shoulders as they lifted into the sky. The sudden whoosh stole her breath and make her insides quiver, not unlike the experience of Drew's lovemaking, now that she thought about it.

She studied his profile as he gazed out the large, curved window. Everything about him was exceptional. He was wildly successful in business, widely liked and respected in Royal. There was even talk that he might be the next president of the Texas Cattleman's Club when Gil Addison's term ended.

The man wasn't perfect. Thank God. Who wanted to live with that? But he was pretty darn close. And he wanted Beth.

Even as she told herself she could adapt to his world, doubt crept in. Audie would never leave her alone if she were married to Drew. He would want money and favors and anything else he thought he could get from his sister married to the big shot. She knew how his brain worked.

Thankfully, the noise of the helicopter meant she didn't have to talk to Drew. After yesterday, last night and this morning, she didn't know what she would say. Maybe she spent too much time worrying, too many minutes trying to predict the future. In the greater scheme of life, there were few things she could control. Not her own destiny, and certainly not the man who was in so many ways her opposite.

He reached for her hand, turning her heart to mush. She had never been much of a girlie girl. No time for hearts and flowers and doodling a guy's name on notebook paper.

But with Drew, she found herself softening, enjoying the many ways he showed her he cared.

He was a man. Arrogant. Always sure he was right. But he gave her something she had never found with anyone else. Not even Richard. Drew gave her the unshakable conviction that she had found the person who was her other half.

It might not be the same for him. It might not be forever. But it was the most exhilarating feeling she had ever experienced.

Leaning into his shoulder, she closed her eyes and dreamed. The helicopter closed the remaining distance to Royal rapidly. Soon they'd be back to life at Willowbrook. And Audie living on her farm. And all the heartaches from the storm. But with Drew at her side, she knew she had the support to deal with whatever came her way.

At last, the pilot set them gently on Drew's home turf. Drew jumped out and reached up to lift her down, his hands lingering a bit longer than necessary at her waist. He kissed her cheek. "You ready to enter the house of crazy?" he asked.

She chuckled. "From everything I've heard, weddings are always a little bit out of control."

"True. But since Jed and Kimberly have invited the entire town of Royal, *crazy* may be only the beginning."

Thirteen

Drew was chagrined to find that his joking description was painfully accurate. The serenity of Willowbrook farm had morphed into a state of total chaos. In addition to Drew's own fairly large staff, several dozen outsiders had converged on the ranch. There were tents to be erected, chairs to be lined up, barbeque grills to be stationed.

And that was only the beginning.

Since Jed seemed to have things under control, Drew spent his time in the stables. Recently, he'd had offers for two of his stallions. The money would help finance the next big expansion. A month ago, that expansion had been all he thought about. After the storm, things looked very different.

To his frustration, Drew barely saw Beth after their return from Dallas. She was swallowed up in the responsibility of being Kimberly's de facto wedding planner, coordinating everything from menu items to the bride's clothing. Kimberly walked around with a beaming smile on her face, nothing at all like the bridezillas Drew had heard about. Jed, on the other hand, was snappy.

Drew caught him by the arm as he passed in the hall. "What in the hell is wrong with you, man? You're acting like a horse with a burr under his saddle."

Jed leaned against the wall, rotating his head and rubbing the back of his neck. "I know this was partly my idea, but God in heaven, I never expected it to snowball like this. I should have kidnapped Kimberly."

"Oh?" Drew tried to remain neutral, even though he was in his brother's court.

"I want Kimberly. That's all."

Suddenly, Drew understood. "You mean you *want* Kimberly."

"Isn't that what I said?" Jed snarled.

Drew managed not to laugh, but it was tough. His brother was suffering from sexual frustration. Kimberly had kicked him out of her apartment in town. Beth was her new roommate as the women took care of final wedding details.

By the same token, Drew had been deprived of Beth's company. As much as he missed her presence in his bed, however, for him it was a temporary relief. With Beth spending the bulk of her hours in Royal, Drew didn't have to worry every minute about her learning the truth about Audie.

Drew was going to confess. Hopefully, she would be grateful that he was helping get Audie back on his feet. He wanted to ease Beth's troubles. That had been his intent all along. He wasn't a liar by nature, and even though he knew Beth was going to be pissed, he had to tell her.

But when the wedding was over....

The day after the Dallas trip was a blur. Everyone had a question for Drew. *What about this? Can we do that? Where will we find those?*

While he was happy to help, no one seemed to acknowledge or care that he had a ranch to run. The pandemonium only increased. Thankfully, by sundown on the eve of the wedding, a brief lull fell over Willowbrook.

At long last, he and Jed kicked back in the den to drink beer and eat steak and baked potatoes. With no womenfolk in the house, they decided to have their own impromptu version of a bachelor party. The meal began in silence as they watched a play-off game on the big screen TV.

Sometime later, Jed set his empty plate on the coffee table. "Thanks, Drew."

"For what?"

"Keeping me sane."

Drew grinned. "I like having you here. You know that. It seems like old times. What does Kimberly think about the move to Dallas?"

"She's excited, I think. The Cattleman's Club there is going to have a reception for us pretty soon after we get back."

"So things at the club are going well?"

"They are. It's not as big as the one here, of course, but we're getting new members all the time."

"Good." Drew put his dishes aside as well. "You want another beer?"

"Sure."

When Drew returned from the kitchen, Jed sat with his elbows on his knees, his head in his hands. Drew put the open beer beside him and resumed his seat. "You okay, baby brother?"

Jed looked up at him, his eyes glazed. "I don't know the first damn thing about being a father. I've tried not to let Kimberly see, but I'm scared, Drew. What if I mess things up? I'm not worried about Kimberly and me. We're solid now. But I'm going to be responsible for a human life."

Drew nodded. "I could tell you it will all be fine, but what do I know? I guess most of it comes instinctively. Like in the animal kingdom."

"True, but that's usually the female of the species.

Human dads in the twenty-first century are supposed to be hands-on."

"I've known you your whole life. You never walk away from a challenge. You've got this, Jed. You and Kimberly. You'll be fine."

The tension in Jed's shoulders visibly relaxed. "You're right. As long as I have her, I've got everything I need."

Beth was exhausted but exhilarated. The morning of Kimberly and Jed's wedding day dawned perfectly. The weather forecast promised blue skies, a light breeze and temperatures in the upper seventies.

Kimberly was sleeping in, so Beth tiptoed around the apartment as she fixed a cup of coffee. She had been taken aback when it became clear that Kimberly wanted to include her not only in the preparations, but also in the small wedding party. Kimberly's lack of family plus the fact that her two best friends from childhood had married and moved far away in the last two years meant that this extremely quick wedding left her with few options for female support.

In a normal situation, with months to plan, her friends would have flown back to Royal, of course. But despite how much they loved Kimberly, it just wasn't possible on such short notice.

So Beth set out to do everything in her power to make this day wonderful for the bride.

As much as Beth was embroiled in last minute details, she couldn't stop thinking about Drew. They had barely seen each other since the helicopter brought them back from Dallas. She knew she had to make some decisions soon. She believed Drew had strong feelings for her. So why did she still have doubts?

All this wedding fever put ideas in her head. She

couldn't deny it. But it was never good to make important life decisions in the heat of the moment. First the storm, and now Kimberly and Jed's baby news. A quickie marriage ceremony. Would life ever get back to normal? Until it did, Beth wasn't sure she could make any kind of commitment to Drew even if he asked.

Two hours later, she and Kimberly loaded Beth's loaner truck with everything they would need for the day. The two of them had put together a detailed list so nothing would be overlooked. Kimberly was pale but calm. Drew had orders to keep Jed occupied while Beth smuggled Kimberly into Beth's suite of rooms at Willowbrook.

On the drive to the ranch, Kimberly stared out the window, her hands resting protectively over her almost nonexistent baby bump.

Beth envied her in many ways. Having a baby was an incredible blessing. Kimberly's sweet spirit would translate well to maternal devotion. Then there was Jed, who so very clearly adored his high school girlfriend. The two of them seemed meant for each other. Which was a statement Beth couldn't make about herself and Drew.

Doggedly, she put her own agenda out of her mind for the moment. This was Kimberly's day. Beth was honored to be a part of it.

Fortunately, they made it inside the house without detection. No bad luck to endure because the groom saw the bride before the ceremony. While Kimberly showered, Beth read through texts and emails on her phone.

One from Drew made her heart race, though it had nothing to do with romance.

Kimberly came walking out of the bathroom wearing a thin robe, a towel in her hand as she dried her hair. "What's wrong?"

Beth realized that her face must have revealed more than she intended. "Um, nothing."

Kimberly sat on the edge of the bed. "I'm not a fragile flower. Tell me what you just read."

Beth bit her lip and gave her the bottom line without dressing it up. "According to Drew, over four hundred people have RSVP'd by phone, text or email that they're coming to the wedding. And that's not counting the ones who will show up without letting us know."

Kimberly's eyes widened. "Oh. My. God. What happened?"

"Apparently your idea worked. People are so overwhelmed and sad and tired from the cleanup, they jumped at the chance to have some fun."

"Is there enough food?"

"Drew says he and Jed have it under control. The caterer is catatonic, but I heard two helicopters land while you were in the shower. Drew and Jed are reveling in the moment, I think. You know. Macho men handling impossible logistics."

"Better them than me."

Beth laughed. "I think you and I have the easy part. All we have to do is get you dressed and walk down the aisle."

The ceremony was scheduled for four o'clock. At twenty till, the housekeeper came to say that all the guests were in place. Many of them, apparently, were perched on hay bales hastily pressed into service for additional seating.

Beth touched Kimberly's shoulder. "You look beautiful. Are you ready?"

Kimberly's lip wobbled. "It was supposed to be casual and fun."

"And it still is," Beth said firmly. In light of the town's tragedy and given the impromptu nature of the nuptials,

Jed and Kimberly had opted for nontraditional clothing. The men were wearing pressed dress jeans with crisp white shirts and bolo ties made from polished petrified wood that had been found on Willowbrook land back in the early 1900s. Hand-tooled boots, of course, completed their rig.

Kimberly had chosen as her bridal gown a simple, strapless, knee-length dress in cream silk and lace. Her only adornment was a stunning strand of pearls Jed had given her as a wedding gift. The elegant jewelry once belonged to his grandmother. Because of the tornado, Kimberly didn't even have an engagement ring, but Jed swore to remedy that as soon as they got to Dallas.

Beth's maid-of-honor dress was Kimberly's choice as well. It echoed the bride's in style, but was a shade of pale green, to complement Beth's eyes.

The two women stared at each other. "We'd better go," Beth said. "Don't want to give the groom a heart attack."

Drew stood beside his brother in front of the minister beneath a trellised arch woven with blush pink roses and gazed out over the guests. In addition to the extended Farrell family, half the town had showed up, it seemed. So many familiar faces dotted the crowd. Nate Battle, the sheriff and his wife, Amanda, who ran the diner; Sam and Lila Gordon, whose courtship had gotten off to a rocky start but who now had a set of twins; Ryan Grant, the rodeo star, and his better half Piper, who worked out of the hospital as a paramedic. The list went on and on. Families Drew and Jed had known since childhood, along with newer friends.

A string quartet had played for a long time as the guests were seated, but now the music changed. The crowd rose to its feet with a murmur of approval. As the notes of Pachelbel's Canon lifted on the autumn breeze, Drew's eyes strained until he saw a familiar figure appear and begin to walk down the endless satin runner.

His heart stumbled to a halt. Beth. She walked toward him with a small smile on her face. Their eyes locked. Something sweet and deep passed between them. The bride followed only a few steps behind, but Drew never saw her. His whole focus was on the woman who had become as necessary to him as oxygen and food.

The dress she wore made her look like a gift of spring, even though the calendar said otherwise. Her hair, shiny and glowing in the sun, floated around her shoulders. The small posy of rosebuds she carried was held at exactly the correct angle.

Everything about her was perfect. At last, she reached the front and took her place opposite Drew.

Vaguely, he was aware that Jed stepped forward and took Kimberly's hand. But Drew continued to stare at Beth, even as the small wedding party turned as one to face the minister.

Later, he couldn't remember a single thing that was said. Vows were exchanged, rings blessed and finally the pronouncement. With the citizens of Royal clapping and cheering, the newlyweds made their way back down the aisle.

At the appropriate moment, Drew took Beth's arm in his. His chest bursting with love and pride, he walked her toward the house, smiling broadly.

Jed and Kimberly stepped inside the ranch house for a moment of privacy. Drew dragged Beth to a sheltered corner of the porch out of sight. "God, I've missed you," he muttered. He wrapped her in his arms and kissed her roughly, rejoicing when she gave him eager passion in return.

"Enough," she said finally, breathing heavily. "We have to go back for pictures."

"Pictures?" He parroted the word, unable to think about anything but getting her naked and under him ASAP.

"C'mon, Drew. It's their day. We can't ruin it."

He understood Beth's point and applauded the sentiment. But a beast raged inside him. Beth was his. He wanted to tell the whole world. And he never wanted to spend a night apart from her again.

Today, however, social convention demanded he live up to his role as host.

What followed was a combination of high spirits, ample food and drink and a celebration of life in the wake of what could have been death for those in the crowd. The tornado had marked everyone in attendance in one fashion or another. There was still much to do. Sorrow had visited households that would need time to recover. But today was about joy.

Hours later, Drew waved as Jed and Kimberly departed via helicopter for their honeymoon. At the same moment, the last of the guests and caterers rolled away in a string of vehicles down the road to Royal. Soon, he and Beth were alone, standing near the front of the house.

The tents and chairs were still up...and the grills. But cleanup would finish tomorrow. Dark closed in.

He reached for Beth's hand, feeling a heady mix of contentment and anticipation. "Alone at last."

The words had barely left his mouth when one of his two top guys approached, his mouth grim. "I hate to bother you, boss. But we've had an incident. Someone left a gate open. Inkblot got out and injured his leg."

Inkblot was one of Willowbrook's prized stallions— worth a couple million dollars, not to mention the stud fees.

"No one on my staff is stupid enough to let that happen."

"It was the new guy."

Beth cocked her head and stared at Drew. "The new guy?"

The foreman responded. "Audie Andrews. He's your brother, right? No offense, ma'am, but I didn't expect him to screw up this fast."

Beth clapped a hand over her mouth, but she was unable to muffle a sound of distress. Drew reached for her. She backed away, her face white. The foreman stood watching them both, a look of confusion in his gaze.

Drew clenched his teeth, damning the timing. "Go get Andrews. I want him in my office immediately."

The foreman strode away at a rapid clip, clearly aware that something more was going on. Drew turned to Beth. "I can explain."

Dull acceptance replaced her look of disbelief. "I told you," she said. "I warned you. Did you not believe me?"

"You weren't specific. He told me about his alcoholism and his six months sober. I assumed you had trouble believing he had changed. I thought if I gave him a job he could prove himself and get his own place sooner. I was trying to *help* you," he said through clenched teeth. "Is it really such a hell of a big deal?"

Beth's eyes flashed. "You tell me. You're the one with a damaged horse. You're so arrogant and bossy you can't bear to stay out of my business. After the storm, I decided maybe I had misjudged you, but apparently not." She whirled and ran for the steps to the house.

"Where are you going?" he shouted, desperation and anger dueling in his chest.

"To pack."

He stalked after her. "And go where?"

Facing him from the porch, she wrapped her arms around her waist. Her eyes glittered with pain. "I have a key to Kimberly's apartment. I'll stay there. I never should have come to Willowbrook at all."

She disappeared into the house. Drew let her go. Once she had a chance to calm down, he could make her see reason.

Beth slung clothes into the bag she had taken to Dallas. It wouldn't hold everything she had brought from her house after the tornado, but she could ask the housekeeper to box up the rest later and send it to Kimberly's address.

She didn't have a plan after that. Embarrassment and anger sent tears rolling down her cheeks as she gathered up her toiletries in the beautiful bathroom. Today had been perfect. Until Audie ruined things. Like he did every other time.

But the weird thing was, Audie wasn't the focus of her fury and disappointment. Audie was simply being Audie. She had learned to expect nothing more from him.

Drew was another story. He had given her a roof over her head so she wouldn't have to live in a half-demolished house. He had made love to her as if she was the only woman on the planet....

But the one thing she asked him to do—stay away from her brother—had apparently been too much. He'd deliberately ignored her wishes. Audie would never have had the initiative to go to Drew about a job. Clearly, Drew had sought out Audie. But why, when he knew what Beth had said about her brother? Because the mighty Drew Farrell always knew best. And he didn't give a damn if anyone else thought differently.

Well, it didn't matter now. This debacle was exactly the reason she didn't belong in Drew's rarefied world. Audie was her brother, and as such, he would always be a millstone around her neck. Even in the short time Beth had stayed at Willowbrook, she had come to understand the value of Drew's horses. The one injured today, Inkblot, was a wildly expensive cornerstone of Willowbrook's breeding program.

Thanks to Audie, the valuable animal had been hurt.

Wiping her face with the back of her hand, she finished packing and debated whether or not she would bother saying goodbye to Drew. Part of her wanted to show him that she was poised and coldly angry. The better decision, though, seemed to be a quick escape.

But she couldn't resist one last chance to see him before she left. Tiptoeing down the hall, she approached Drew's office. If he was finished reprimanding and probably firing Audie, perhaps she would say something. But as she drew closer, she realized that her brother was still with his boss.

She eavesdropped unashamedly.

Drew spoke sternly. "I gave you a chance, Andrews. And you blew it."

"Somebody's trying to pin this on me, Mr. Farrell, I swear. I never left that gate unlocked. You gotta believe me."

"One of the men saw you leaving the stall area just before the wedding."

"Yeah, that's true. One of my buddies from town wanted to see your horses. I guess I'd been braggin' a little about workin' here. So I took him back for a look. But that's all we did, I swear. I know it was a dumb thing to do."

Silence reigned for a few seconds. Then Drew spoke again. "Beth tried to warn me about you, but I thought she was overreacting."

Audie's angry voice ricocheted off the walls. "She never

gives me a chance. Nobody does. And for a rich guy, you aren't too smart."

Beth leaned against the wall just outside the door and put a hand over her eyes. Audie was an idiot with a bad temper.

Drew's voice could have frozen lava. "Not that I really care, but would you like to elaborate on that remark?"

"My sister," Audie yelled. "She's playing you for a fool. And it isn't the first time. She's already had one sugar daddy bail her out. Now, after the tornado, all she had to do was bat those long eyelashes at you and suddenly, she's tucked up in your little palace here being treated like a queen. I know she's sleeping with you."

Moments later Audie wailed.

Beth couldn't help herself. She peeked into the room and saw Drew nursing his fist. His chest heaved, and his face was flushed with anger. Audie lay flat out on the floor with a giant purplish red spot on his cheekbone.

Drew looked up and saw her standing there. Everything inside Beth melted in despair. She'd been the one to tell Drew about Richard. Now, Audie's vindictive accusation painted her in the worst possible light.

She ran.

Out of the house. To the battered pickup truck. Down the road to town.

As she drove, hands shaking on the steering wheel, humiliation choked her. Her budding relationship with Drew was too new to withstand this wretchedly embarrassing incident with her brother.

Even worse, maybe Drew thought she had lied about her relationship with Richard. Maybe in light of Audie's words, Drew thought Beth had *used* Richard. And now was using him.

Glancing in the rearview mirror, she stepped on the gas

a bit harder, half expecting at any moment to see Drew's vehicle hot on her heels. But the road was empty.

In Royal, she headed for the only place guaranteed to provide refuge. She holed up in Kimberly's apartment and cried. By nightfall, she accepted the truth.

Drew was done with her. How did she know? He didn't try to follow her. He had let her go without protest.

And that was the cruelest blow of all.

Three days later, she finally attained a fragile state of calm acceptance. It helped that the insurance money had come through. She'd hired a contractor, and with a professional's help, began making the string of decisions that governed the remodeling of her home.

But she conducted all meetings in town. Until Audie was off her property, she was not going back there. And she surely wasn't going to risk a run-in with Drew. Not under any circumstances.

Deep in one little hopeful corner of her heart, she believed he would come for her. That tiny bit of positive energy told her he would eventually understand that she had given him her heart…that she didn't sleep with every man with money who came along.

But the hours passed, and Drew didn't come.

At the seven-day mark, she regretted looking in the mirror. She hated being a pitiful, grieving mess. Each morning she forced herself to dress and put on lip gloss and mascara so she could pretend to the world that she was normal. But it was only an act. She ate barely enough to keep from starving. Her stomach hurt from bouts of sobbing. The tears came at night when there was no one else to see. Desperation lurked with each new sunrise.

Kimberly and Jed were returning to Royal tomorrow afternoon. Though they would soon be moving to Dallas, they planned to stay at Kimberly's place in the meantime. Neither of them knew Beth had moved out of her room at Willowbrook.

Beth couldn't be in residence when the newlyweds came home.

But where was she to go?

Every motel and hotel and B&B in town was full of refugees from the storm. She knew. She had checked.

That night she packed her things. The weather was still pleasant. If she drove out toward the interstate, she could park at the rest area and sleep in the truck. It was a plan, but not much of one.

It took her two trips to load her stuff into the cab. She had accumulated a small stash of food. The cooler she purchased yesterday would keep it edible. She shivered when she realized that her preparations exhibited a sad familiarity. Once more she had been reduced to living as a nomad.

With one last look around to make sure everything was spic and span, she took a deep breath and told herself she could exist without Drew.

She had lived self-sufficiently and by her wits for a long time, remarkably so after her troubled upbringing. No need to suffer a broken heart simply because one man didn't want her like she wanted him. Another day, a fresh start. First on the list was a trip to the local furniture store to buy a new kitchen table and chairs. The manager promised to hold it for delivery until the contractor had finished the repairs.

Picking up her keys and her cell phone, she opened the door.

Drew stood on the sidewalk.

He watched the color drain from her face. It was some small comfort to see that she had suffered as much as he had. His stupid mistake had started the whole mess, but Beth had been the one to cut and run without fighting for what they had.

"Hello, Beth," he said quietly.

Her expression was hunted. "I have an appointment," she said, the terse words just short of outright rudeness.

"Let's get something straight. I knew you were here the whole time. But I thought we both needed some time to think."

"There you go again. Assuming you know what's best." The comeback lacked her usual heat.

"Jed and Kimberly are coming home tomorrow."

"I know. That's why I've moved out."

"Moved out to where?"

"None of your business."

He studied her intently, noting the changes. Though she had lost weight after the storm, now her cheekbones were even more sharply defined. She wore jeans and a casual shirt, looking much like the woman who had battled a tornado with him.

She scrunched her eyes against the sun and pulled out a pair of sunglasses. "I really have to go," she said.

Now he couldn't read her gaze at all. He took one of her hands, disturbed to find it ice cold. Did she despise him? Had his careless actions, his lack of respect for her feelings cost him everything?

"Please," he said urgently. "Give me one hour. Then if you still want to go, I won't stop you. In fact, I'll never speak to you again if that's what you want."

He saw the way her throat worked. Recognized her agitation in white knuckles and beautiful lips pressed in a firm line.

"Why?" she asked, her voice sounding dull.

"Because I need to apologize."

"So do it."

He held on to his patience. "I'm sorry for not listening to you about Audie. But I can't believe you thought I would let his nasty allegations sway me."

She took off the sunglasses, her eyes stony and blank. "They were true. Every word."

"So you don't love me?"

Her jaw dropped and her eyes widened. "That's ridiculous."

"Am I supposed to believe that the only reason you had sex with me was so I would give you room and board? That's absurd. I *know* you, Beth. And I choose to believe that you feel something for me. Don't you? Just like I feel something for you. Something I'm pretty sure is love."

He cupped her cheek, ignoring her move to evade him. "I'm sorry, Beth. Sorry for everything. Sorry I didn't have the courtesy to listen to your opinions and preferences. Sorry that I gave you so little confidence in our relationship that you had to run."

Finally, she spoke. "Why did you wait so long to come find me?"

He tugged on her hand. "One hour. Please. I want to show you something."

That she accompanied him was a miracle. But maybe she thought it was the only way to be rid of him. He had brought a car, not his truck this time. In the trunk he had a few necessities in case things went his way, but mostly he wanted her to be comfortable.

He opened the passenger door, helped her in, then ran around to his side, not entirely sure she wouldn't bolt.

Unwilling for her to guess his intentions, he drove around several blocks in town before heading out toward Willowbrook. When it was time, he turned onto Beth's road.

When he reached the edge of Beth's fields, in sight of her house and the storm cellar, he stopped the car and helped her out.

He led her toward what used to be her produce stand and positioned her with gentle hands. "Take a look."

Beth blinked in astonishment. Her flattened produce stand had been rebuilt. The structure still smelled of new wood. A jaunty, brightly colored sign announced "Green Acres—Good Food at Good Prices." Even more astonishing were the piles of pumpkins artfully arranged. Dozens of pumpkins, maybe hundreds.

Artificial fall leaves and real corn shocks decorated every available space.

"I don't understand," she said, thinking the whole thing must be a mirage.

Drew stood shoulder to shoulder with her, his hands shoved in his pockets. "I want you to be happy, Beth. Even if it's not with me. I've tried to reset the clock to the day before the storm hit. I wasn't able to put the pumpkins back in the field for photo ops, but you're all ready to reopen whenever you want to."

She bent down and picked up a mini pumpkin, its color the perfect orange. "I don't know what to say." When she stood again, she stared at him face-to-face for the first time. He looked worse than the day they had both survived a killer tornado. Shadowed eyes, grim lines around his mouth.

He took her hands in his, forcing her to meet his eyes. "Audie is not staying here anymore. I made him help me with all this, and then I booted him out of your shed. He says he wants to apologize to you for all the things he said that day in my office. But I told him it might be best to wait a little bit. I wasn't sure you could handle seeing him yet."

"Angie and Anton?"

"I found them an apartment. They moved this morning."

"He won't appreciate your kindness the way he should."

"I did it for you."

When her bottom lip trembled, she bit down on it. Hard. "How is your horse?" She had worried about Inkblot every day.

"He's doing well. And I think you should know, Audie is still working for me. It turns out he was telling the truth."

"Then who left the gate open?"

"One of the wedding guests. A horse-crazy thirteen-year-old girl. When the family got home that night, the daughter confessed she had been sneaking around my stables. She went into Inkblot's stall to pet him, but the stallion scared her and she ran. She knew she had left the gate open. The father called me and apologized."

"Did you tell him the horse was injured?"

"No. I didn't want to make him feel worse."

"Well, I'm glad it wasn't Audie."

"Tell me what you're thinking," Drew said, gently brushing a strand of hair from her cheek.

She flinched. And saw him suffer.

He backed away. "God, Beth. I'm sorry. I know you don't want to hear it, but I love you. I'm sorry I went behind your back."

She lifted her shoulders and let them fall. "I don't care about that anymore. But don't you see...?" She paused, her throat thick with tears. "Audie will never go away. If I agree to a relationship with you, he'll be an embarrassment to your business and to your family. I can't be responsible for that."

"Because why?"

"Because I love you, too. And you deserve a wife with some family credentials. Someone who knows how to plan a dinner party for three dozen people or at least a woman who can tell one end of a thoroughbred from another."

He grinned. "You are such a snob."

She frowned. "I certainly am not."

He pulled her close and kissed her soundly, ignoring her halfhearted attempts to escape. Finally, he held her at arms' length. "The only wife I want is you," he said, breathing heavily, his gaze intent. "If you turn me down, I'll be a pitiful, aging bachelor with no one to love me."

She brushed her fingers over his lips, wondering if happiness really was in reach. "You are such a scoundrel." Closing her eyes, she nestled against him with a smile, resting her head on his chest and feeling his heart beating beneath her cheek. "But what about Audie?"

"I can handle your brother, Beth." Drew's big hand was warm on her back. She soaked in the moment, unwilling to rush ahead when anticipation was so very sweet. Arousal and exhilaration danced in her blood.

Apparently, her patience was greater than his. "Now what do you say to my proposition?" he asked.

"Have you actually posed a question yet?" She could feel his impatience in the way his body shuddered against hers.

Without warning, he went down on one knee, looking up at her with such naked love it made her chest ache. "Beth Andrews, will you marry me?"

The sky was bluer, the breeze sweeter, the sun as warm and perfect as the love in her heart. She feathered her fingers through his hair. "Yes, I will. Under one condition." She pulled him to his feet. "I want to offer you a wedding gift."

"Okay." He appeared mystified.

"A man like you has everything. So I'm giving you Green Acres."

He shook his head instantly. "No, Beth. I can't take your farm. I can't bulldoze the roots you've worked so hard to put down. This is important to you."

She went up on tiptoe and kissed him, lingering long enough to feel her pulse race as his arms tightened around her. "*You're* important to me, Drew. I want to make babies with you and learn the horse business and be a part of Willowbrook. Those are my conditions."

The stunned shock in his blue eyes gave way to mischief. "How soon can we start on the making babies part?"

"I'd like a ring on my finger, first. You Farrell men are so darned impulsive."

He picked her up in his arms and carried her back to the car. "Did I mention I have a blanket in the trunk? And a picnic?"

"I love you, Drew." She kissed his chin.

"And I love you, my stubborn, beautiful Beth. It may have taken a killer storm to bring us together, but I'm never letting you go."

"I can live with that."

And so she did...

* * * * *

Texas Cattleman's Club: After the Storm
Don't miss a single story!

REQUEST YOUR FREE BOOKS!
2 FREE NOVELS PLUS 2 FREE GIFTS!

ALWAYS POWERFUL, PASSIONATE AND PROVOCATIVE

She hurried down the steps, then remembered she was trying to make a good impression. She slowed too quickly and stumbled. Hard. She braced for the impact.

It didn't come. Instead of hitting the floor, she fell into a pair of strong arms and against a firm, warm chest.

Whitney looked up into a pair of eyes that were deep blue. He smiled down at her and she didn't feel as if she was going to forget her own name. She felt as if she'd never forget this moment.

"I've got you."

He did have her. His arms were around her waist and he was lifting her up. She felt secure.

The feeling was *wonderful*.

Then, without warning, everything changed. His warm smile froze as his eyes went hard. The strong arms became iron bars around her and the next thing she knew, she was being pushed not up, but away.

Matthew Beaumont set her back on her feet and stepped clear of her. With a glare that could only be described as ferocious, he turned to Phillip and Jo.

"What," he said, "is Whitney Wildz doing here?"

Don't miss
A BEAUMONT CHRISTMAS WEDDING
By Sarah M. Anderson

Available November 2014 from Harlequin® Desire.

What if Matthew Beaumont could look at her without
caring about who she'd been in the past?

What if—what if he wasn't involved with anyone?

Whitney didn't hook up. That part of her life was dead
and buried. But…a little Christmas romance between the
maid of honor and the best man wouldn't be such a bad
thing, would it? It could be fun.

She hurried to the bathroom, daring to hope that
Matthew was single. He was coming to dinner tonight
and it sounded as if he would be involved with a lot of the
wedding activities.

Although…it had been a long time since she'd attempted
anything involving the opposite sex. Making a pass at the
best man might not be the smartest thing she could do.

Even so, Whitney went with the red cashmere sweater—
the kind a single, handsome man might accidentally brush
with his fingers—and headed out. The house had hallways
in all directions, and she was relieved when she heard
voices—Jo's and Phillip's and another voice, deep and
strong. Matthew.